WINE COUNTRY COURIER

Community Buzz

It seems that our wrongly accused Grant Ashton is doing an awful lot of running—to the side of one Anna Sheridan, that is. Who can blame him? After all, she did jump to his rescue and tell the world that he couldn't have commited Spencer Ashton's murder because he was with *her* at the time. And it's not like she didn't have a lot to lose. Anna is raising her late sister's son, and I'm sure she would never do anything that would threaten her custody of the little boy. It certainly will be exciting to see what happens next between the prodigal son and the mistress's sister.

But here's the big surprise…. Sources have confirmed that Spencer's estranged daughter, Grace Ashton, and her husband have been located. That can only mean trouble for the Ashtons. And for Grace's twin brother, Grant. Because she has been nothing but trouble for that man. You can be sure this compelling story will continue to get more and more juicy!

Dear Reader,

It's November and perhaps the weather is turning a bit cooler where you are…so why not heat things up with six wonderful Silhouette Desire novels? *New York Times* bestselling author Diana Palmer is back this month with a LONG, TALL TEXANS story not to be missed. You've loved Blake Kemp and his ever-faithful assistant, Violet, in other books…. Now you finally get their love story, in *Boss Man*.

Heat continues to generate in DYNASTIES: THE ASHTONS with Laura Wright's contribution, *Savor the Seduction*. Grant and Anna shared a night of passion some months ago…now he's wondering if they have a shot at a repeat performance. And the temperature continues to rise as Sara Orwig delivers her share of surprises, in *Highly Compromised Position,* the latest installment in the TEXAS CATTLEMAN'S CLUB: THE SECRET DIARY series. (Hint, someone in Royal, Texas, is pregnant!)

Brenda Jackson gets things simmering in *The Chase Is On,* another fabulous Westmoreland story with a strong emphasis on food…tasty! And Bronwyn Jameson is back with the conclusion of her PRINCES OF THE OUTBACK series. Who wouldn't want to share body heat with *The Ruthless Groom?* Last but not least, get all hot and bothered in the boardroom with Margaret Allison's business-becomes-pleasure holiday story, *Mistletoe Maneuvers.*

Here's hoping you find plenty of ways to keep yourself warm. Enjoy all we have to offer at Silhouette Desire.

Best,

Melissa Jeglinski

Melissa Jeglinski
Senior Editor
Silhouette Books

Please address questions and book requests to:
Silhouette Reader Service
U.S.: 3010 Walden Ave., P.O. Box 1325, Buffalo, NY 14269
Canadian: P.O. Box 609, Fort Erie, Ont. L2A 5X3

SAVOR THE SEDUCTION
Laura Wright

Published by Silhouette Books
America's Publisher of Contemporary Romance

Special thanks and acknowledgment are given to Laura Wright for her contribution to the DYNASTIES: THE ASHTONS series.

This book is dedicated to all of the Ashton Ladies. You are the best. And to MJ, for giving me this opportunity in the first place.

SILHOUETTE BOOKS

ISBN 0-373-76687-4

SAVOR THE SEDUCTION

Visit Silhouette Books at www.eHarlequin.com

Printed in U.S.A.

Books by Laura Wright

Silhouette Desire

Cinderella & the Playboy #1451
Hearts Are Wild #1469
Baby and the Beast #1482
Charming the Prince #1492
Sleeping with Beauty #1510
Ruling Passions #1536
Locked Up with a Lawman #1553
Redwolf's Woman #1582
A Bed of Sand #1607
The Sultan's Bed #1661
Her Royal Bed #1674
Savor the Seduction #1687

LAURA WRIGHT

has spent most of her life immersed in the world of acting, singing and competitive ballroom dancing. But when she started writing romance, she knew she'd found the true desire of her heart! Although born and raised in Minneapolis, Laura has also lived in New York City, Milwaukee and Columbus, Ohio. Currently, she is happy to have set down her bags and made Los Angeles her home. And a blissful home it is—one that she shares with her theatrical production manager husband, Daniel, and three spoiled dogs. During those few hours of down-time from her beloved writing, Laura enjoys going to art galleries and movies, cooking for her hubby, walking in the woods, lazing around lakes, puttering in the kitchen and frolicking with her animals. Laura would love to hear from you. You can write to her at P.O. Box 5811, Sherman Oaks, CA 91413 or e-mail her at laurawright@laurawright.com.

THE ASHTONS

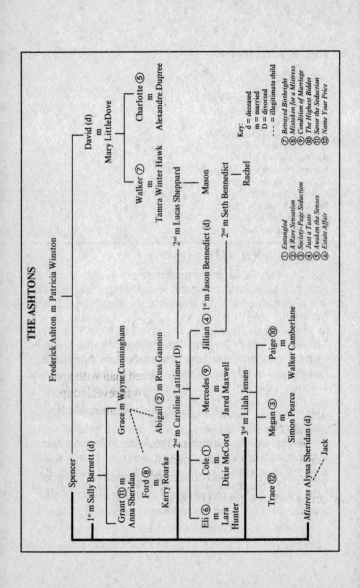

Frederick Ashton m Patricia Winston

Spencer

1st m Sally Barnett (d)

Grace m Wayne Cunningham

David (d)
m
Mary LittleDove

Grant ⑪ m Anna Sheridan

Ford ⑧
m
Kerry Roarke

Abigail ② m Russ Gannon

Walker ⑦
m
Tamra Winter Hawk

Charlotte ⑤
m
Alexandre Dupree

2nd m Caroline Lattimer (D)

2nd m Lucas Sheppard

Cole ①
m
Dixie McCord

Mercedes ⑨
m
Jared Maxwell

Jillian ④ 1st m Jason Bennedict (d)

Mason

2nd m Seth Bennedict

Eli ⑥
m
Lara Hunter

Rachel

3rd m Lilah Jensen

Trace ⑫

Megan ③
m
Simon Pearce

Paige ⑩
m
Walker Camberlane

Mistress Alyssa Sheridan (d)

Jack

Key:
d = deceased
m = married
D = divorced
- - - = illegitimate child

① Entangled
② A Rare Sensation
③ Society-Page Seduction
④ Just a Taste
⑤ Awaken the Senses
⑥ Estate Affair

⑦ Betrayed Birthright
⑧ Mistaken for a Mistress
⑨ Condition of Marriage
⑩ The Highest Bidder
⑪ Savor the Seduction
⑫ Name Your Price

Prologue

On the eighteenth floor of the Ashton-Lattimer building located in San Francisco's Financial District—in a very spacious, though sparsely furnished executive office—sat a silver-haired man with green eyes and a lean, athletic build that was revealed spectacularly well in one of his many custom-made Italian wool suits.

As always, he sat behind the Andies Grey marble desk he'd had specially made five years ago, the fingers on his right hand drumming meditatively beside the phone as if he were eagerly awaiting his next call, while the fingers on his left hand caressed his chin.

It was nine-thirty in the morning, and he should've been working. But his foolish secretary had allowed an unwelcome visitor inside his inner sanctum. His mouth slipped into a frown. He did not want her here, and it irritated him beyond measure to have the control he so frequently enjoyed stripped from him.

But it would return, he assured himself.

And soon.

"Spencer, we need to talk."

Contempt snaked through his blood as Alyssa Sheridan ran a hand over her flat belly. Dressed in plain virginal-white, her long auburn hair pinned back in a bun, she looked the part of a disadvantaged woman. Her large brown eyes were liquid with tears as she gazed at him. At one time, he'd thought she was beautiful. Now, even in her prim attire, she looked used.

His lips twisted into a cynical smile as he leaned back in his black leather armchair. "What is it you think those crocodile tears will get you, Alyssa?"

She stopped biting the inside of her cheek and released a breath. "All I want is for you to be a father to this child."

"I have enough children."

"Surely you have room in your heart for one more."

"I have no heart," he said matter-of-factly.

"Spencer, please—"

"I am Mr. Ashton here," he cut her off with a sneer, then eyed her belly. "How do I know that it's my child you're carrying?"

A muscle quivered in her jaw. "Of course it's your child." She shook her head. "I haven't been with anyone else."

"So you say. You fell into my bed easily enough."

She made a slow, sallow sound, like a whimper. "I don't understand this."

"What is it you don't understand?"

"Where's the man I knew? The man I thought cared about me, wanted to take care of me—the man I fell in—"

"Stop right there." He leaned forward, whispered menacingly, "Let's not mistake a few nights of sex for anything more than the minor distraction that it was, shall we?"

She went white as the walls. For a long moment she said nothing, then she lifted her chin a fraction and said softly, "What about your wife? Maybe she'd like to know about your little…" Tears pricked her eyes once more. "Distraction."

He chuckled sardonically. "How clever of you to think of that, but alas, my wife is fully aware that I dip my pen in a few other inkpots from time to time."

"And she's supportive of that kind of behavior, is she?"

He stiffened with arrogance at the question. "Let's just say, she can't do anything about it. No one controls me." He raised one sharp eyebrow. "No one."

Tears fell onto her cheeks, but all that concerned Spencer was where they would fall next. If she leaned forward, even an inch, his desk would be directly below her chin, and salt could be tricky on marble.

"If there's nothing else…" he began hastily.

"Just this." She swiped at her eyes. "You're a bastard, Spencer Ashton."

He snorted. "Perhaps I am, but if you don't get rid of that—" he gestured to her belly "—you'll be caring for your own little bastard soon enough, and with absolutely no help from me."

Her hands flew to her stomach as if to protect the life growing there from his words.

"Goodbye, Alyssa," he said casually, his gaze returning to the files on his desk. "And if you try to break into my office again I'll have you arrested."

He didn't look up until he heard the door slam. But when he did, he smiled.

One

Red curls, large green eyes and a smile to make you weak.

"Love you, Mama."

And then there was that, Anna Sheridan mused, her heart melting as she opened her arms to her boy.

Her boy.

She'd gotten entirely too used to calling him that. True enough, he wasn't her son. He was her nephew, her sister Alyssa's child. But her sister's death, and the baby's father's lack of interest, had forced Anna and Jack together—had tragically, though wonder-fully, made them mother and child from the first day of his life.

Of course, Jack was too little to understand the

truth behind their relationship, but Anna knew that someday she would have to tell him. Right now, she thought as he came flying at her, pouncing on her with one of his all-encompassing, orange-Popsicle-flavored kisses, she was just going to protect him, love him and mother him the best way she knew how.

Anna glanced heavenward. Alyssa was watching over them both, making sure Anna was giving Jack the life he deserved. It was only right. Regardless of her indiscretions, weaknesses and faults, Alyssa was a good person at heart, and she would've wanted only the best for her child. No doubt she had expectations of Anna, and Anna would meet them, gladly, happily. After all, she'd always managed to follow others' expectations of her. A lifetime of expectations.

But, of course, with Jack, being the best she could be was a pure pleasure.

"Run, Mama?" Jack asked her hopefully, his eyes wide and full of excitement.

Anna smiled. There was nothing Jack loved more than running, except maybe pizza, and he was awfully lucky to have such an amazing expanse of space to indulge in that love. Well, maybe not lucky. For Anna and Jack, it had been a necessity for them to come and stay at the Vines. After the media had gotten wind of who Jack's father was, they hadn't let up on Anna. They wanted their questions answered and had gone to ridiculous lengths to gain an interview.

And then there had been the threats.

Anna shivered. Thank goodness for Caroline and

Lucas. They had been truly wonderful, amazingly generous—as had Jack's half brothers and sisters. Everyone at Louret Vineyards had showered Anna with support, while making sure Jack had a ton of attention.

Anna and Jack hadn't been staying there for too terribly long yet, but already her sweet toddler was completely at home at the Vines. His mother, on the other hand, had never felt so unsure of herself, and had never felt so beholden in her life.

From her spot on the blue woolly blanket underneath a beautiful oak, Anna gazed out over the rolling hills of Louret Vineyards, the amazing French-style home, the small lake and stables, and the lush sixty-five acres of vines. Growing up the way she and Alyssa had, in a one-bedroom apartment with cheese sandwiches for both breakfast and dinner, she could never have imagined that a world like this existed. And, unlike her sister, had never sought it out. All she'd wanted to do was better. And thankfully, through education, through her beloved teaching, she had.

"Run, Mama? Run," Jack repeated.

"I'm sorry, love. Mama's a little under the weather today." Anna hated to deny him anything, but she just wasn't herself today. Her stomach had been churning since breakfast, and she felt really exhausted. "But I have a ball. I can throw it and you can run and get it and bring it back to me."

This seemed to appease him, and he chanted, "Ball, ball, ball," until she finally tossed it over the grass.

Jack sure did love it here. Surrounded by space and wildlife and more family than he could count. It wasn't going to be easy for him to leave when Spencer's murder was finally resolved, to return to their cramped apartment in the city.

She paused, her heart squeezing. It wasn't going to be easy for her to leave, either. True, she wasn't as at home here as Jack, but there was something—someone she would miss very dearly.

Despite the crisp November day, heat moved through her body, and she wondered if the cause was the coming fever or the thought of the man who dwelled in her thoughts 24/7. She glanced past Jack and swallowed tightly. The man who was walking toward her at this very moment. The tall, self-possessed man with a crop of dark brown hair and hooded green eyes—the man who made her forget her name with just one touch.

Her heart dropped piteously into her weak stomach and continued to sit there and pound away. Dressed in a pair of worn jeans and a blue-flannel shirt he looked slightly out of place in the fancy vineyard landscape. But the supreme confidence that hummed from him stated differently. This man belonged wherever he wished. On this vineyard, driving cattle, driving a tractor or making love to a woman who adored him.

Yes, Grant Ashton looked impervious now, as he picked up Jack and tossed him in the air, but it wasn't always so. Just a few months ago, he'd been locked up in a San Francisco jail, his freedom revoked. Both he and Anna had wondered if he'd ever see daylight again. His confidence had surely waned during that precarious time, and Anna had felt his pain and fear in her soul. That's why, despite his command that she keep their night of passion a secret, she'd told the police exactly where Grant had been the night of Spencer Ashton's murder.

In her bed.

Grant handed the ball back to Jack and headed over to Anna. Despite her aches and waves of weakness, she longed to jump up and run at him, wrap her arms around his neck, her legs around his waist. But she remained where she was. Over the past few days, she'd been avoiding him. Not because she didn't want to be with him. But over the last several weeks, as time passed and her feelings grew stronger, she'd realized that she needed to start protecting herself. When he left California for his home in Nebraska, her heart was going to bleed.

The thing was, they'd gotten too close, too fast. Making love to him, curling herself up in his arms, talking about nonsense and matters of importance to them both had become addictive. So when that dreadful, unavoidable day did come, she didn't want to hate him for leaving, hate herself for allowing things to go even further, having expectations of a future that he'd never offered. A future he couldn't even think about right now with Spencer Ashton's murder still in the forefront of his mind, life and soul.

A bout of exhaustion came over her, adding more weight to her already queasy stomach. "Jack, hun, we should get going soon. It's almost time for your nap."

"Bird, Mama. Birdie," Jack squealed, pointing to a tree branch, completely ignoring her suggestion.

"I see it, baby. It's blue, right?"

"Blue, blue."

"Yes, baby."

"Gwant, Gwant, Gwant," shouted Jack, now pointing at the man in front of her.

"Yes, baby," she said, staring up into eyes that she'd seen tender, hot, unsure and humor-filled, but never as they were right now—irritated.

As Jack went to inspect the birdie in the tree, crunching over brittle brown leaves, Anna mustered up a friendly, noncommittal smile. "Hey, Grant."

But he didn't return the easy welcome. He wasn't a man to mess around. He got to the point whether you wanted to go there or not. "Are you avoiding me?"

"No," she lied.

"No?"

"Well, not exactly."

"Not exactly?" He hunkered down next to her, and as they talked they watched Jack play with his ball. "C'mon, Anna. You know I don't like games."

"This isn't a game."

"Then what is it? What's going on?"

With an enormous exhale, she flipped up her hands. She wasn't all that good at small talk and avoidance, either. "I wanted to give you some space, that's all."

"Space for what?" he asked darkly.

"To work out your feelings regarding your family, and the situation surrounding your father's—"

"Please don't call him that," Grant muttered tightly.

"Sorry. I just thought you might need some breathing room."

"Well, I don't. And I don't have any feelings to work out, either."

She sniffed. "I don't believe that."

"Why? Because I'm still hanging around Napa?"

"For starters."

"Dammit, Anna. You know I can't go until Spencer's murder is solved. The cops won't let me and I won't let myself."

She despised the severe dip in her heart at the main reason he remained at the Vines. Of course he wasn't staying for her. She had to get a grip and realize they were only having an affair—and a short-lived one at that. "I've got to go," she said, her head feeling suddenly heavy as a rush of chills raced up her spine.

Grant studied her. "You look a little gray."

"Thanks," she said, coming to her feet, zipping her sweater all the way up to her chin.

He stood quickly and helped her. "Are you sick?"

"I'm fine. Just tired."

He looked as though he didn't believe her, looked as though he knew her better than that. "I need to see you later."

The chills were coming in daunting waves now. She needed to lie down. "What for?"

"Do I really need a reason, Anna?"

His green eyes moved over her face—not in a sexual way—but in a restless, desperate way.

"Listen, Grant," she began, her patience, her pride and her thin veil of self-preservation dropping away as all her energy went to combat her chills and rocky stomach. "For a while, I was willing to be that soft place for you to fall. But my feelings for you are getting stronger and…well, I'm afraid."

"Of what?"

"Spinning my wheels. You know how I feel about you. I'm plain as day when it comes to that."

"Anna…"

"I know you have a huge weight on your shoulders right now. The last thing you can think about is where a relationship is going. But I can't help thinking of it. I'm a woman who wants a future for me and my son, and you're…not…" *What? Ready? A man in love?*

He held her shoulders gently. "I'm sorry, Anna. I wish I could give you what you need—what you deserve." He shook his head. "God knows I do, but right now—"

"You don't need to say it—and honestly, I don't need to hear it."

He nodded, then released a weighty breath. "Family's a strange thing, you know? Too many surprises, too many damn secrets."

"I know."

His gaze sunk into hers, wouldn't let go. "I have Spencer's blood in my veins. Doesn't that scare you a little?"

"No," she said matter-of-factly.

"It sure as hell scares me."

"You're nothing like him, Grant," she said, easing herself from his grasp.

Looking frustrated, and very confused, Grant muttered, "I don't know who I am anymore."

"I know," she said, wanting to comfort him, but remaining as impassive as she could. "But you have to figure that out."

He paused, his jaw working. "Without your help, is that what you're saying?"

"That's an incredibly selfish question."

The lines in his forehead deepened. "I'm afraid I'm a selfish bastard when it comes to you." He reached out, touched her face. "You're a good woman, Anna."

Her skin tingled under his touch. Or maybe it was the chills. "I've got to go."

"Let me help you."

"No." She stood tall, tried to look less feeble. She didn't want Grant to know how sick she felt. He'd insist on coming over, helping her, putting her to bed. He was such a nice guy that way. But she couldn't handle his gallantry right now. She needed to get her heart under control.

"I think we should take a break from each other

for a while," she said, then quickly moved away from him and toward her child. "Let's go, Jack."

"Bye-bye, Gwant," Jack said as he was tugged off toward the cottage.

"Bye, Jack. I'll see you later." His voice turned deep and serious. "I'll see you both later."

As Anna walked away, as she fought every quiver and quake in her belly, every squeeze of her heart, she pretended she hadn't heard that last bit.

Grant brought the stallion to a sharp halt. Sure he'd made skid marks in the dirt, he glanced down, but there was nothing, nothing but hoofprints and animal tracks.

Boy, it felt good to be on a horse again, he thought, letting his stallion prance in a circle. Made him feel alive and free, the wind in his face. But the scents in the air were different, and no matter how hard he tried, he couldn't pretend he was on his land in Nebraska and away from speculation and controversy. No, this was California country, Caroline's land—the one thing Spencer hadn't taken from her.

Spencer Ashton.

The name made Grant cringe, made his fist tighten around the leather strap in his hand. That man had caused so much grief to so many people, yet from that grief and web of lies, he'd brought many people together. The irony had Grant chuckling sardonically. Did he thank the ghost that had introduced him to siblings he now considered friends? Did he thank

Spencer's memory for making Jack or bringing Anna into his life?

He gave the stallion a light kick and urged him to walk through a wide row of grapevines. He had no answers to such complicated questions. His life in Nebraska had been so simplistic, so steady, predictable, no surprises. He could appreciate that now.

But then again, Nebraska lacked many things: his half brothers and sisters; his little brother, Jack and Anna Sheridan.

Tall, thin, with brown leather eyes so large and liquid a man wanted to drown in them. Never had a woman captivated his mind and body like her, he mused as the sun set casually before him. And he was pretty sure she felt the same about him. Hell, hadn't she said as much? But unlike him, she wanted a relationship, a father for her boy and a husband for herself. And Grant Ashton, this new Grant Ashton that was made just months ago, this Grant Ashton who had been lied to, taken advantage of, abandoned by his father and tossed in jail for a crime he hadn't committed, had no stomach for commitment. Besides, he'd seen way too many people end up hating each other over a love gone wrong, over unsure futures and selfish choices. And he'd seen too many kids torn apart in the process. Himself included.

He wasn't going to risk that with Anna and Jack.

But, hell, he thought, emerging from a row of vines and breaking into a canter across an open patch of land, even with all those good reasons to steer clear, to follow her wishes and stay away, he couldn't stop himself from wanting her.

"Pardon the cliché, but I'm truly sick as a dog."

Standing in the cottage doorway, Jillian gazed at her friend with concerned eyes. "What can I do?"

Wrapped in a blanket, feeling insanely hot and cold at the same time, Anna said, "I don't want Jack to get this, whatever it is. Can you take him up to the house for tonight?"

"Of course," Jillian said, then gestured to Anna. "But who'll take care of you?"

"I've nursed myself out of the flu too many times to count. I just want Jack to be all right."

"He'll be fine. Rachel is so excited she's ready to burst. And so's the rest of the clan." Jillian studied Anna's face. "Please let Caroline bring you some soup or toast or—"

"I'm okay. I have soup and bread and Popsicles. Caroline is a busy woman, and has been wonderful to me. I don't want to be a burden."

Jillian rolled her eyes in an, "Oh, for heaven's sake" type of look. "Promise me this, okay? If you start to feel really bad, you'll call?" When Anna didn't answer, Jillian pursed her lips and warned, "That boy of yours needs his mother."

Anna attempted a smile. "Okay. I promise."

"Good," Jillian said, pacified.

"Come here, Jack." Anna moved aside and let the little boy through. Jack took the hand Jillian offered him, but looked up at Anna with sad eyes. "Mama?"

Her heart tripped, and if she didn't feel like something that had been caught in a drain, then promptly battered and fried, she'd take her baby in her arms and never let go. But desires had to come second to her boy's health. "Just one night, love. I promise."

"'Kay," he said softly, then smiled. "Wuv you."

"Love you, too, baby."

After he and Jillian left, walking off toward the house, Anna closed the door. For a moment, she sagged against the wood, feeling depleted and incredibly lonely. She didn't know what ached more, her bones and muscles or her heart.

After pushing away from the door, she staggered over to the couch and collapsed onto the fluffy white pillows. Her muscles aching, her stomach churning, she pulled one of Caroline's beautiful quilts up to her chin. The movement was exhausting. Lord, it was going to be a long night.

The kitchen clock ticked away as she lay there trying to urge herself to drink fluids. After a few sips of water, she let her eyes drift closed. For what seemed like hours, she moved in and out of sleep, waking up when a supreme dose of cold or heat rushed up her spine. Shaking sadly, sweat beading on her brow, she wished someone would conk her on the head and put her out of her misery for a while.

She groaned when she heard a knock on the door,

but then forced herself to rouse when she realized it could be Jillian and Jack.

But when she pulled back the cottage door, she got a surprise. Grant stood there, the twilight to his back, a scowl on his handsome features.

"You really are sick."

"It would seem that way." She knew she looked like hell, but she didn't care.

"You said you were fine, just tired."

"Did I?"

He ignored her sarcasm. "Why the hell didn't you call me?"

"You know why."

"I'm coming in."

"No."

"Yes."

"Grant, I can handle this, it's just a bug."

He lifted one very serious brow. "Are you going to step aside or do I have to pick you up?"

"You're being ridiculous," she said.

"And you're being a stubborn child."

She felt ready to wilt right there, and stepped back to allow him entrance. "No, what I'm being is practical and protective." She leaned against the wall as a wave of nausea hit her.

He cursed, eased her from the wall and into his arms. "You don't have to protect yourself from me, ever."

The nausea moved like ocean waves in her gut. He just didn't get it. Of course she had to protect herself. Unlike him, she was in love and ready to have her heart broken whenever he was able to leave Napa.

"My poor, Anna," he whispered against her hair.

His voice was soothing, and he felt so cool and strong and just what the doctor ordered that she allowed herself to relax against him.

"This isn't a good idea," she muttered against his brown leather coat.

"You're sick, Anna."

"I know."

"So apart from applying a cold cloth and feeding you soup, I'll keep my hands to myself, okay? Just let me help you."

Her neck felt so tight, her bones ached terribly. Could she? Could she just allow him to help her for one night?

A shot of liquid cold snaked up her spine, then spread.

Yes, tonight she could.

"What are you feeling?" he asked her gently, guiding her back to the couch.

She collapsed on the soft, familiar fabric. "Hot and cold, chills, hot, sick to my stomach, cold and weak."

He sat on the coffee table, pulled the quilt up to her chin. "Did you eat something funny?"

"I don't think so. It's probably just the flu."

He stared at her for a moment, then his brows dipped low and his voice followed. "Anna?"

"What?"

"Are you sure this is the flu?"

"What do you mean? Of course it's the—"

"Well," he began slowly, taking her hand in his, "we were together almost a month ago. The weakness, nausea…"

Oh, for goodness' sake. She shook her head. "Grant—"

"It all makes sense."

"Not to me," she said, her heart pinching under aching ribs.

He leaned toward her, his eyes a brilliant green mask from whatever emotion he was feeling. "Could you be pregnant, Anna?"

Two

His life flashed before his eyes.

All forty-three years.

From birth to now. From his fatherless childhood, to a mother who worked her hands raw and her feet into a nightly salt soak just to keep clothes on their backs and food in their mouths. From grandparents who had given them all a home, to his mother's battle with cancer, to his rebellious sister Grace who, after the death of their mother, went wild and careless and gave birth to two children—and finally to the leap into parenthood when Grace had abandoned those children.

Grant's gaze slipped from Anna's bleary brown eyes to her belly. He had become an adult, a father—a parent—early and quickly. And even with all of the trials and setbacks, he'd managed to raise two amazing people.

Yet, he wasn't sure he could do it again.

He wasn't sure he wanted to do it again.

"Grant."

He looked up, back into Anna's soft gaze.

"You can unclench that jaw. There's no baby."

"How can you be sure?"

"We were always careful."

"Things happen. Condoms break. Especially when two people get a little wild."

"Just a little?" She tried to smile, though it looked almost painful to do.

He leaned toward her, stroked her hair. "You look really pale."

"You gotta stop flattering me like this."

He chuckled, leaned in and gave her a kiss on her damp forehead.

Admittedly he was a responsible guy. He did the right thing most of the time, had the respect of his friends and workers. Made sure the job was done and done right, no matter how long it took. But when it came to nursing, to caretaking, for someone other than himself, he had pretty meager instincts. Sure, he'd been there for his kids when they'd been sick, stayed up all night, held their heads, held them close, whatever they needed. It was those other things; singing, soothing with words—all that stuff that seemed to come so easy to a woman, to a mother.

When he looked down into the face of this woman

he wanted to have all manners of soothing on hand. It was like that with Anna. He felt merely a man with her, when he wanted to be everything and give her everything.

"You're too close, Grant."

"What?"

"You'll get sick, too."

"Nah." He grinned, eased a wisp of auburn hair off her cheek and gazed down at her. "And what if I do? You can take care of me."

She closed her eyes, shakes hitting her full-on now. "Oh, Grant. How…will we…stay apart if…"

He shook his head. "You need to lie down."

"I am lying down."

"No, not properly. You need a bed."

"Bed would be good. But it's too far away."

"Not so far," he said softly, sliding his hands under her and lifting her up, blanket and all.

"Listen, Grant," she said weakly as he carried her toward the bedroom. "I appreciate your help, but I'm really capable of taking care of myself."

The two cuss words that fell from his mouth were followed up by an imperious, "You're weak and sick. If you are…well, carrying a child, especially in the early months, that can make you—"

She looked up at him, said with much more vigor than she probably possessed, "I am not pregnant."

Maybe she was, maybe she wasn't, he thought, pulling her closer in his arms. But he wasn't taking any chances. "We'll see."

"I just don't want you to worry about it, not with everything that's going on right now—"

He laid her on the bed. "I'm not worried."

But Grant was worried. For many reasons. His bloodline was riddled with people who ran from their responsibilities. Sure, he'd proven himself once. He'd raised Ford and Abigail, and had always been proud of that fact, not to mention proud of them. But things had changed—he'd changed—since he'd come to Napa Valley. Spencer's rejection, his murder, his lies about the past. Grant's arrest and Anna's cover-up. The deceit that surrounded him was abundant, making the future look bleak and unsure.

There were times when Grant wondered what kind of man he had become.

He glanced down at Anna. She was asleep, her cheeks flushed with pink, her breathing labored. His chest constricted as he pulled the loose blanket up to her chin. Despite all of those other concerns, there was one far more powerful and troublesome. If Anna were carrying his child he would be bound to her for life, and the idea both excited and terrified him.

She wrapped her arms around her child as she ran through the alley. Someone was following her, slowing when she slowed, quickening his pace when she sped up. Her heart thundered in her chest and her forehead dripped with sweat. She was so exhausted, and her baby couldn't keep up as they hurried through the long unending tunnel of darkness.

At one point, she tripped on something wet and hard. Down she went, Jack with her. Panic rose in her blood and she forced herself up, forced herself to pick up her child and run.

She could feel the man's hot breath, smell his sickeningly sweet cologne.

"Go away," she shouted, her breathing heavy, the bullets of sweat dripping down her forehead to her cheek. "He's mine. Mine!"

His breath came quickly, too, as he remained one step behind her.

The hair on her neck bristled and bile rose in her throat.

"You'll never have him. Don't touch him!"

"Anna! Anna?"

She screamed and struggled with arms that bound her.

"Anna, wake up."

Anna's eyes flew open. She was sitting up, her heart thundering inside her chest, her face wet with perspiration. She blinked, swallowed, then stared, unfocused, into green eyes. Wide, concerned eyes.

"Grant?" she whispered, then released a cry of relief and let her head fall against his chest.

"Yeah." Grant cradled her. "You were having a nightmare."

"It was him again."

"Spencer?"

"He was taking Jack from me."

"It's all right now," he assured her, stroking her

hair, holding her as tightly as she'd allow him. "He can't hurt you ever again, and he will never take your child from you."

"It won't die. This dream won't die. Why couldn't it die when he did?" Spencer chasing her, wanting to take her baby from her. Over and over. Night after night since this whole thing began. The last time she and Grant had been together, under very different circumstances of course, she'd woken up screaming, panicked from the same dream.

She wiped the sweat from her hot forehead. "Oh, God. I have a fever."

"I know." He grabbed a bottle from the bedside table and turned it over, shook out two caplets onto his palm. "Here, take these."

"What is it?"

"Just take them."

Too exhausted and too sick to argue, she did as he instructed, then gulped down the water he offered.

Heat, unlike anything she'd ever known, settled over her and she felt as though she couldn't breathe. Her mind a blurry, bleary mess, she started ripping off her clothes.

Grant stared at her. "What—?"

"Hot. So hot." But she barely had her shirt over her head when weakness took her and she sagged against Grant's chest.

"Let me, sweetheart."

Through her fever haze, she thought she might have smiled. She loved when he called her that. It had only been three times, twice during lovemaking, and once tonight. She wished it could be always.

With deft fingers, Grant lifted her T-shirt over her head, then snapped the hooks of her bra and removed it from her scorching skin. He laid her back against the pillow, and eased down her pajama bottoms and underwear at the same time. She sighed as air rushed over her skin.

But the cool and comfortable feeling lasted for about ten seconds.

Goose bumps rose on her skin and she thought she would be sick to her stomach if she didn't get warm. "Now I'm freezing. Oh, and every bone, every muscle in my body aches. Even my hair hurts."

Grant pulled the covers up to her chin, tucked her in at the sides. "Better."

"No. So cold." Her teeth began to chatter, and she wondered bleakly if she could die from the flu. As a teacher, she knew that there were some pretty grim statistics regarding flu deaths.

From ever so far away, she heard the whiz of a jeans zipper. She opened her eyes, saw through fuzzy vision and the dim light from the hall lamp that Grant was removing his clothes.

"What are you doing?" she asked.

"Getting in bed with you."

"Grant, I can't…not tonight…I—"

"Just keep quiet now," he commanded gently. "You'll feel better in a second."

He crawled in beside her, pulled her back into his

chest and wrapped a protective arm around her. Anna released a breath. Heat, good and solid seared into her, and she pressed back even further against him. She felt his shaft against her backside, felt it grow thick and hard, but she didn't care. She was warm and almost comfortable for once.

"Sorry about that," he muttered.

"Don't apologize."

"Being this close to you…"

"It's all right." A quick shiver moved through her and she sucked air through her teeth.

His arm tightened around her. "Sleep now, sweetheart."

The heat and his endearment took hold of her sick body and weary mind and allowed her to relax, allowed her to move into a deep and dreamless sleep.

It was 3:00 a.m. and Grant had just given Anna some more Tylenol and soothed her back to sleep. He was starting to believe that what she had really was a bad case of the flu. He was no doctor, but chills and fever didn't go hand in hand with pregnancy, surely.

He expected relief to fill him at the realization, but strangely, it didn't.

Beside him, Anna shuddered. He kissed her hair, then closed his eyes, put his head to the pillow and tried to go back to sleep. But sleep didn't come. His hand itched. Wanted to move. Wanted to explore. Not in a sexual way, but in an emotional, proprietary way that made him apprehensive as hell.

His hand rested lightly on her rib cage, but quickly slipped lower, until it brushed over her flat belly.

Something close to grief invaded his soul, and he felt confused and ashamed for wanting something he shouldn't want or have.

But he didn't pull away.

He fell asleep like that, his chest to her hot back, his erection to her round buttocks and his hand on her belly.

Three

Sunlight bounced off the trees outside the cottage window and lazily crept into her room.

Anna took a deep breath, filled her lungs with the fresh air of reality and subsiding illness and released it, slowly and easily. She felt better. Not one hundred percent, but the fever was gone, she was terrifically hungry and her body no longer ached.

Well, not from the flu, at any rate.

Beside her, a man slept, his big, tan, lean-muscled body tangled in the sheets, his dark brown hair mussed and his chin rough and sexy with shadow.

Anna cuddled into her pillow and smiled. She remembered his heat last night, and the evidence of his desire for her pressing into her lower back. But she also remembered his goodness, his friendship and care. Sure, Grant Ashton could be stubborn and demanding, but he was also the most giving, tender man she had ever known. If he could just let go of Spencer's hold on him—the past's hold on him—if he could just let go of his fears, maybe he'd take a chance and embrace her and the life they could have together.

Without consideration, she reached out and brushed her thumb across his mouth. He didn't stir and she let her fingers move to his jaw, down his neck to his collarbone, then into the light sprinkling of hair on his magnificent chest.

"Keep going and I'll have to forget how sick you are," he uttered, his dark lashes pulsating as he forced one eye open.

She laughed softly. "Did I wake you?"

He grinned. "Of course you did."

"Sorry about that."

"No you're not, and neither am I."

She smiled, looked into his hot eyes and wished she had a permanent place there.

"How are you feeling?" he asked, running a hand up her arm to her shoulder.

"Better."

"You sure?"

"Don't I look better?" she teased with a fond smile. "No more pale, gray, drawn—"

"You look sexy is what you look."

"Really?"

"And if I don't get out of this bed, I'm going to have to do something about it."

"Like what?" she asked, laughing.

He grinned. "Don't press your luck."

She whipped back the covers, wrapped her leg around his waist and hoisted herself toward him. His hard shaft pressed against her feminine curls and she whispered, "I think I'm pressing my luck."

His eyes were filled with a red-hot gleam. "You think?"

"I am. I definitely am."

His hand raked up her thigh, found her backside and squeezed. "You're crazy, Anna Sheridan."

"You have no idea."

She wrapped her arms around his neck, leaned in and kissed him. It was a soft, slow kiss that drugged her, made her unable to breathe for a moment. Back and forth her mouth brushed over his until he groaned and tightened his hold on her backside. Heat surged into her core at the slight pain and pleasure he inflicted, and she ground her hips into his erection.

Grant followed her, his lips hardening like the rest of him as he kissed her passionately. He was a man of great passion, but he hid it all too well. There was nothing Anna loved more than when he showed that devilish, roguish side of himself to her and only her.

"Mmmm," she uttered, her body melting as she stroked his legs with her own.

"I know," he murmured against her mouth, then swiped her lower lip with his tongue.

"More?"

"Yes."

His kiss went deep, angled, plundered and she bucked against him, clung to him, wished for more, wished for him to dive inside of her. A shallow swat of dizziness came over her, but she willed it away. After all, she hadn't eaten for close to twenty-four hours. All she needed was a little sustenance. And Grant was supplying all the nourishment she required.

As his lips fed on hers, Anna could feel his heart beating inside his chest, could feel that rapid pulse against her breasts. She wondered if he wanted to be inside her, too, wanted to taste her, wanted to go faster and slower and have more and more.

Then he suddenly left her mouth and dipped his head, found her breast. Anna gulped for air as he flicked his tongue back and forth over her nipple. Her breasts ached, her core ached. Her heart slammed in her ribs, and her inner thighs and feminine hair were wet with need.

Grant rolled onto her, and his hand slipped between her legs as his mouth found hers once again. Her hips stiffened and rose as his fingers found her, stroked the bundle of nerves at her core where she burned desperately. Anna had always thought of herself as passive and cautious both in bed and out, but Grant made her wriggle and squirm and participate in her own pleasure, demand and accept, and love her femaleness.

He slipped a finger inside her and she gasped, her

legs jerking, the muscles in her thighs flexing. He used the wetness of her body to slip in and out and slowly circle over the swollen bud at her center.

She looked up. He was watching her, his green eyes glittering rabid fire. She knew those eyes, and God help her, she loved the man behind them. If only he felt…

Her thoughts died as he plunged two fingers inside her, deep, all the way to the knuckle. Her hips thrust, her hands fisted around the wrinkled sheets. White-hot strands of energy ripped through her, and she cried out, heat and pulse and fireworks erupting within her.

"Anna, sweetheart," Grant said soothingly as he held her tightly. "I'm desperate here."

Her body pulsed, weak from hunger, weak from delicious torture. And yet, she wanted more. "Come inside me," she whispered, her breathing ragged, her hand moving down his torso, searching for his shaft.

"No."

"What?"

"Another time."

"Grant…"

He kissed her, eased her hand from his throbbing penis. "Anna, last night and this morning was about you, making you feel good. Okay?"

"No, not okay."

He sat up. "There'll be plenty of time…"

Anna wanted to say, *"Bull"* to that. There would not be plenty of time. Maybe a few more nights, a couple of glorious weeks. Who knew for sure? He was going back home soon, back to his life.

She watched him slip on his jeans and shirt, his jaw working with the unleashed passion she knew flooded every cell of his being. "Where are you going?" she asked.

"I have an appointment."

"With who?"

"One of Spencer's employees."

Shock slammed into her. "You're going to San Francisco?"

"Yes."

She sighed, feeling a nagging sense of worry replace the ardor from a moment ago. "Grant, why can't you let the police handle this?"

"Because I can't."

"What if you get in trouble—?"

He walked over to her, looking determined and impatient. "Listen, Anna, I can't do a damn thing until I'm cleared of this murder."

"Like what? Go back home?"

"Yes."

A sharp stab of pain entered her heart. "How about making love to me again? Is that on hold, too?"

His jaw tightened. "I told you what that was about. You're just getting over the flu."

She bypassed his lame excuses and got straight to the heart of the matter. "Why do you need to do this? You've been cleared of Spencer's murder."

"No, I haven't. I have the cops watching me, and,

sure, my brothers and sisters have been great, but I see how they look at me sometimes—or try not to look at me."

"That's ridiculous. They're all wonderful to you."

"They're only ninety-five percent sure I'm innocent."

"I don't agree. That sketch the police showed us and the whole blackmailing thing, it's cast a new light on this investigation."

"Not a *new* light, but maybe a different one. It's just something I've got to do, okay?" And with that, he leaned down and kissed her.

For a few sweet seconds, he remained close to her face, waiting for her to return his kiss or smile or give him some sign that she supported him and understood.

Anna would always support him and he knew it. She smiled, reached up and touched his face. "Good luck. I hope you find something of value."

The tension vanished from his eyes, and he kissed her once more. "When can I see you again?"

"Tonight?" she said.

He grinned. "What happened to me giving you some space?"

Yes, what had happened to that self-preserving notion? It had gone out the window the minute he'd climbed into bed naked, his warm, strong body next to her weak and shivering one. "*I* never wanted the space. I was doing it for you."

"Well, stop it already," he admonished playfully.

She couldn't help herself, she laughed. She was

weak and careless, and practically asking for her heart to be broken, but this was Grant and she loved him. How was she supposed to ignore that fact no matter how little time was left? "So, tonight? Dinner?"

"You sure you're up to it?"

"I'm sure."

"Why don't I bring something—"

"No." She sat up, the sheet to her breasts. "I feel more energetic than I have in three days. I want to cook."

He smiled. "I love your cooking."

And I love you.

"I'll be back by six," he said, dropping one last kiss on her mouth before heading out the door.

Anna threw off the covers, her head a little heavy and her body still pulsing from climax and a wonderful, though strange, night and morning that had ended far too soon. She sent good thoughts with Grant as she heard the front door close, and hoped he found nothing more today than his way back to her.

It was selfish, she knew, but she didn't care. She wanted him safe, his body, his mind and his soul, and she truly worried that if he found something new digging around in Spencer's company it might only damage him further.

"You have his eyes."

If he heard that one more time, Grant thought darkly, shifting in his seat, he was going to put his fist through a wall. As if having the same eyes as his father would be all that strange. Of course, maybe the comment was more of a cover-up for deeper thoughts, tricky questions about what else the two men had in common, comments that couldn't be said while trying to remain polite.

"Not the expression, mind you, but the color."

Across from Grant, sitting behind a thin mahogany desk in a very small windowless office on the top floor of Ashton-Lattimer Corporation, was a man in his late thirties with a hook nose and deeply-set blue eyes who yesterday had agreed to meet with Spencer's eldest child. He'd been the only employee who'd agreed to see Grant.

Young Pritchard patted his thinning hair and gave Grant a tight-lipped smile.

"The expression?" Grant repeated.

"Well, you do have the seriousness of the late Mr. Ashton, but...well, the arrogance isn't there."

Spencer, arrogant? Grant mentally rolled his eyes. What he needed was information he'd never heard before. Maybe an offhanded remark about a worker who had a grudge, or something to hold over Spencer's head, something the police missed in their formal interviews.

"You know," Young said, leaning forward as though he had something delicate to discuss, "he spoke of his firstborn, his eldest boy many a time."

"Is that right?" Grant said tightly, not sure he really gave a damn.

"Of course, I always thought he was talking about

Caroline's boy." He shook his head. "Who could've guessed…"

"Spencer was a walking enigma," Grant said. "Though I doubt he was talking about me. I'm sure it was Eli or Cole."

Those small blue eyes narrowed. "You have a sister, don't you? A twin."

"That's right." Grant paused. He didn't talk about Grace very much, and was surprised that Spencer had mentioned her.

"Then he was talking about you. Fairly recently actually. Kind of 'off the cuff' one day. Mirror images, he'd said, but nothing alike."

A muscle worked in Grant's jaw.

"Actually," the man continued, "he called her a chip off the old block, but it didn't sound like a compliment."

What a shocker, Grant thought sarcastically.

This was going nowhere. He wanted answers, clues to who had hired that sketch artist, who'd paid the kid to frame Grant, and who the hell had been blackmailing Spencer and why. He'd made a mistake in coming here. Odds were this clown only wanted to check out another one of Spencer's many children, and Grant was not about to act the part of a circus freak.

"Is there anything more you can tell me?" he asked Young.

The man had the good sense to look guilty. "No, afraid not. Sorry about that."

Grant stood up, shook Young's hand and said generously, "Thank you for seeing me."

"Good luck to you, Grant. And sorry about your father."

"Yeah," was all Grant could muster.

Five minutes later, he stepped into the elevator and rode it down to the ground floor. He knew that Detective Ryland was outside, parked far enough away to see his comings and goings and to follow him back to Napa—after he'd sent one of his flunkies to question the employees about Grant Ashton's visit.

Anger and frustration seeped into his bones. He had no information and an unwanted escort for the drive back. He wanted to jump on a plane headed east, home to Nebraska where he belonged. Back to what he knew and understood. Back to a place that was simple and had family he'd always known and cared for. Yes, that sounded good.

Yet, then again…

A woman crept into his mind. And a little boy, too.

Even if he had the choice, he just couldn't leave them. Not yet.

The wind off the Bay blasted him as he stepped onto the sidewalk. He spotted the detective trying his damnedest to look invisible in his unmarked car and gave him a quick wave.

She'd walked into town, to the small market with the freshest produce. On her kitchen counter sat beautiful greens, tomatoes, basil and garlic for pesto, chicken and a basket of apples.

It was a homey sight that made her smile.

Back in her cramped apartment and nonexistent kitchen in San Francisco, she'd tried to make a home for herself and for Jack, a place that felt warm and inviting despite its size. And she'd succeeded to some degree. Decorations and familiar knickknacks filled the space, but that hadn't been enough. With her full-time teaching job, life had been pretty hectic, and homemade meals had been few and far between. They'd had pizza once a week and take-out Chinese on Fridays, while Anna had scrambled to invent something exciting out of pasta and cream of mushroom soup for the remaining three nights.

The life of a working mother wasn't easy or idle, but in her case, it was survival.

But happily the weekends would come along, and she'd have Jack all to herself, playing, singing, reading and cooking him those homemade meals.

Anna took out twelve perfectly shaped green apples and began coring and peeling them. She flipped on a little light jazz, looked down at her boy, who was contentedly reading on the floor, and smiled. Life in Napa had been wonderfully different, and she knew she had to savor every moment. Since being here, she'd chopped and minced and baked and stewed to her heart's content. Sure, she missed teaching, but she was teaching her son every day and there was nothing that compared to that.

"Mama?"

"Yes, baby."

His eyebrows raised. "Book?"

Anna smiled. She had always made a point to stop whatever she was doing when Jack asked her to read. She sat down next to him and patted her knee. He grinned widely and curled up into her lap. *The Big Red Barn* turned into *The Very Hungry Caterpillar,* and when she was closing in on *Brown Bear, Brown Bear* little Jack's eyes started to droop.

After putting him down for a nap, she went back to work on her pie. She was just crimping the edges of her butter crust when there was a soft rap on the door.

She wiped her hands on her apron and headed for the living room.

"Hey, you're back early," she said to a somber-looking Grant.

He shrugged. "Traffic was a breeze. How are you feeling?"

"Perfect."

He smiled, leaned toward her and brushed his lips over hers. "Yeah, you are."

She laughed softly.

"How's Jack?"

"He's good. Taking one of his power naps."

Grant pressed her back against the door frame. "So, we're sort of alone."

"Sort of."

The weight of him, his knee between her legs, felt too good and she inhaled deeply. He leaned toward her, and she thought he was about to kiss her again, but instead he let his head fall to her chest.

"It's good to be back here," he said.

"Little chaotic in the city?"

"Always."

"The trouble is, you're a country boy who needs his wide-open spaces."

He nuzzled her neck. "That's right, ma'am."

She shivered, and her breasts tingled. "Well, you'll be back on the farm in no time, I'm sure of it."

Anna mentally begged him to deny that, but he didn't have the chance. Jack's little cries of, "Mama. Mama. Mama," had them both stepping away from each other.

"Not so much power in that power nap," Grant said with a grin.

"The unpredictability of children."

"I remember. It's pretty great, isn't it?"

She loved that he saw things the way she did. "Yes, it is."

Grant grinned. "I'll go and get him."

When Grant returned from Jack's bedroom, he held the small, sleepy boy tightly in his arms. They all went into the kitchen, and while Anna finished crimping the edges of the pie, the boys watched.

"This kitchen is wonderful," she said breezily.

Grant looked around, his gaze skeptical. "A little small if you ask me."

"Small? Are you kidding?"

"In my house the kitchen is twice this size with a fireplace and two ovens."

"A fireplace?" she asked, awe threading her tone.

"Sure. Winters get pretty cold. Got to have a place

where you can sit, have a cup of hot coffee and watch the snow come down."

"Of course you do," she said on a laugh.

Jack fussed to get down and Grant put him on the floor with a bunch of plastic containers and blocks. "Then there's the pot rack, wine storage and a long window box greenhouse for plants and herbs and such."

"You're just torturing me now," she said, giving him a glare of mock severity. "Oh, and I bet after you have that wonderful meal prepared in one of those wonderful ovens and you sit by that killer fireplace, there's a beautiful, magical snowstorm raging outside—and of course this is all on Christmas Eve."

"Of course." He grinned and shrugged nonchalantly. "Got to have a white Christmas."

"Oh, I'm so jealous I could spit."

He laughed. "Not on the pie if you please."

She laughed with him.

He came up behind her and placed his hands on her waist. "I always thought California girls were too thin-skinned to handle a Nebraska snowstorm."

"Not this California girl, honey. Just take me home and I'll show you what a thin-skinned girl is really made of."

She stopped breathing, and slowly glanced over her shoulder at him. All that big talk was just that— big talk, a tease, but there was seriousness in his gaze. And she longed to ask him what he was thinking. Yet, she also dreaded the answer. So she turned back to the counter and said, "The chef must finish here or no one's getting dessert."

His hands came off her waist in a shot. "We can't have that. Jack, you want pie, right?"

"Yum," Jack called.

A few minutes later, Anna looked down and saw Jack and Grant playing on the kitchen floor with the Tupperware containers, blocks, wooden spoons and measuring cups. They were making forts, doing boy stuff and she had to swallow the lump in her throat. She was in domestic heaven, and she couldn't help but wonder what would've happened if she really had been pregnant. Would Grant have wanted them? Wanted a family? Would he have gone so far as to ask her to marry him?

She turned back to the counter and swallowed the tightness in her throat. Just like Grant's love, pregnancy was an impossibility for her. It killed her to recall what the doctor had told her last year—that her chance of having children was virtually nonexistent.

She slid her pie into the oven, and soberly announced, "Not to worry, boys. The pie's in the oven. Now, it's on to the chicken."

"Bak bak," Jack shouted, hitting his Tupperware with a spoon.

"I bet Grant has chicken on his farm, Jack."

Grant nodded. "Maybe a few."

She smiled down at him and just wanted more of today, more of this temporary heaven. "Tell us more about Nebraska."

Four

About a half hour later, as Anna worked on her chicken and pesto dinner, Grant enjoyed that lazy end of the day feeling with his little brother. He rolled the ball down an easy slope, then watched Jack chase after it with pure glee. He watched with a tenderness he hadn't felt in a long time as the little boy stopped, picked up the orange ball and held it up for Grant to see. Grinning, Grant hooted and hollered and clapped his hands.

It reminded him of the early days with Ford and Abigail. He chuckled in spite of himself. He'd been as green as a bullfrog back then, hadn't known a thing about kids except that he'd been one. But he'd learned pretty quick. Just one year in and he could make a great peanut butter sandwich for one child, while telling a funny bedtime story to the other. He learned to never complain, even on those days when he'd wanted to pull his hair out. He learned that he could stay up all night with two sick kids and make them feel loved and safe and cared for. It had been the hardest job in the world—and the best job in the world.

"Hey there."

Grant looked up, saw Eli coming toward him and gave his half brother an easy wave. Eli was a good guy, a friend when Grant had needed one. He was also pretty big, and Grant couldn't help but think that he could just as easily fit in with the men who worked Grant's farm back home as he did working at Louret as head winemaker.

"How's it going?" Grant asked as Eli approached.

But his brother never answered as, all of a sudden, Jack came barreling into Grant and gave him a huge hug around the legs.

Eli laughed. "You could be a football player with that tackle, Jack."

"Ball, ball, ball," Jack repeated, throwing his orange ball at Grant. "More, more."

The men laughed, and Grant tossed the ball down the little hill for Jack again. He squealed and took off toward it.

"You need some serious energy to keep up with him," Eli said.

"Yeah. Good thing Anna's got serious energy."

"How is Anna, by the way? I heard she was sick."

With a shrug, Grant said, "Over the worst of it, she says."

Eli's green eyes narrowed. "She says?"

Grant shook his head. "No. I believe her. She seems fine, and she looks great—beautiful actually." He paused, eyed Eli's growing smirk and knifed a hand through his hair. "What I mean is she's not so pale."

"Right." Eli placed the bottle of wine he'd had tucked under his arm onto the small picnic table beside Grant. "And how about you? Holding up all right?"

"Sure."

"This whole mess will get resolved soon. The will, Spencer's death and all the family squabbles— all of it. And then things will return to normal."

Grant snorted. "Normal? What the hell is that?"

"I have no idea."

Grant chuckled as Jack brought the ball back. He turned to Eli, raised a brow. "So, you up for a little soccer?"

"With my brothers?" He nodded. "You bet."

Eli's words made Grant's chest tighten. For what seemed like forever he'd been alone, an only child. If he was honest with himself, he'd admit that Grace had been no sister to him. But now things were different. He had family—and they seemed to really care about him, what happened to him and how he was doing. He was reluctant to embrace them—just now, at any rate—because he was still a suspect in Spencer's murder. He still felt watched and judged, even though he wasn't. The situation confused him. He didn't know who he was anymore or where he belonged—or to whom he belonged.

Grant watched Eli kick the ball to Jack, who squealed loudly and kicked it back a few inches.

"Kids got a winning foot," Eli said, making for the ball.

"Wonder where that comes from," Grant said. "Any idea?"

"Mercedes had a pretty mean kick when she was Jack's age. I remember the bruises."

As they passed the ball back and forth, they talked and joked about nothing in particular. It was a relaxing, memorable moment of pure guy time that Grant really enjoyed, and he sort of forgot about the time—until he heard Anna's voice calling them in to dinner.

Grant picked up Jack, then turned to Eli. "Do you want to stay for dinner? You could run back and pick up Lara? Share that bottle of wine with us?"

"Maybe another time. Looks like Anna wants her men to herself tonight."

Grant chuckled lightly. "No, it's nothing like that."

Eli flashed him a rare grin. "Sure it's not. See you guys later."

"Yeah, later," Grant said with mock vexation.

Eli tossed them both a wave and took off back to the main house, and Grant and Jack went in to dinner.

Three lullabies, a little rocking, a soft kiss on the forehead and Jack was off to dreamland.

Anna crept out of his room and headed into the living room. Grant had lit a fire in the fireplace, and had placed two pieces of her apple pie on the coffee table. He sat on the couch, his shirt open at the collar, his jeans molded against his muscular thighs. When he caught site of her he smiled and motioned for her to come over and sit beside him.

The scene was beyond inviting. A happy, sleepy baby in bed, she and Grant relaxing together after a long day. A little pie, a little conversation, a little romance.

She could almost forget that none of it would last.

Almost.

With a soft smile affixed to her lips, she sat down beside him on the couch and curled her legs up under her.

Grant handed her a small china plate that contained a rather large slice of pie. "You did a lot of work today. You sure you feel okay?"

"I'm sure."

"We don't want any relapses." He picked up his fork, grinned at her. "Or maybe we do."

"That's a very selfish attitude," she chided.

"I warned you. When it comes to you, Anna Sheridan, I'm a thoroughly selfish man."

"What are we going to do about that?"

He shrugged, took a bite of pie. "Wow! You're one helluva cook."

"Thank you," she said, her manner remaining light. "I can clean, sew, cook. I like most sports and can pretend I like the others."

"Wow…"

"Yeah. Think I'll make some man a good wife?" She was joking of course, and up until now Grant had followed along, but he didn't look amused anymore.

He looked solemn.

He put his uneaten pie on the table and sighed. "You're an amazing woman. Any man would be lucky to be with you."

Rather than trying to return to the playful intentions she'd originally had, she spoke truthfully, though casually. "Well, the most important thing to me is making sure that Jack's taken care of. I think he deserves a family and a father—and I'll probably have to consider that at some point."

"Of course you will. Every kid deserves a family, and two parents if they're lucky." Exhaling heavily, he leaned back against the fluffy couch cushions. "When my sister walked out on her kids, they were pretty young but they understood they'd lost their mother and their sense of family."

Anna couldn't imagine such a thing. "That's horrible."

"It was hard. No kid should have to give up family." Beside her, his jaw was tight as he spoke, his body, too. "They asked for her every day for two years."

"Oh, Grant." She took his hand, laced her fingers with his.

"I was a kid myself really. I had no idea what to do. I just tried to love them a lot, give them the family they deserved—and try to be the best father I could."

"And you were, still are." He'd never opened up to her this way, this much. She wanted this intimacy to continue, for them to comfort each other. They had such similar pasts, similar siblings that cared for little but themselves, then left others to pick up the slack. Yet, they both had deep guilt running through their veins. "A great father and a great brother. I wish I could've been as strong."

His brows knit together. "What are you talking about?"

"Alyssa. If I could've protected her better—"

"Anna—"

"She was an unthinking, unreliable person, but she had a good heart underneath it all. I truly believe that, and I keep thinking that if I could've kept her from Spencer, things wouldn't have—"

Before she could finish her thought, Grant grabbed her hand. He pulled her off the couch and ushered her out of the room. Outside the door to Jack's bedroom, Grant put a finger to his lips, then silently led her in. The bright moon squeezed through the thin cracks in the blinds, dimly lighting a jagged pathway to the crib.

When they were standing beside the baby's bed, Grant pointed to the beautiful, sleeping boy, curled up with his beloved brown cat and whispered, "If you *had* kept her from Spencer, you wouldn't have him."

Anna's eyes went hot, her throat tight as she stared

down at her little Jack. There was nothing whatever to say in return. She swiped tears from her eyes. Grant was right, so right, and she vowed then and there to never allow such thoughts to enter her mind. What had happened had happened for a reason, and the choices that Alyssa had made were her own.

Quietly they stepped out of the room. But they didn't return to the living room. They stood there in the dimly lit hall and looked at each other.

"Thanks," she whispered.

"For what?" he whispered back, his face deliciously close to her own.

"Reminding me about what's really important. The future and the now—not the past."

"Yeah, well, it's something we both need reminding," he said, staring at her mouth intently.

"I'm doing my damnedest to remind you, Grant." The warmth off his body soothed her, made her feel tired and turned on and ready for bed.

"I know."

"But you've got to let me."

"Oh, Anna." He let his head fall back for a moment. "I can't forget a past that is still haunting me."

Silence filled the air between them. Standing with her back to the wall, with Grant's hard, long body just inches from her, Anna's heart pounded in her chest.

"I'd better head out," Grant said, his gaze returning to her.

She nodded, doing her best to look impassive. "Okay."

"I don't think it's a good idea for Jack—"

"Of course."

She waited for him to move, to back off and walk out.

But he didn't.

"You didn't finish your pie," she said stupidly.

"Save it for me?" he asked, his gaze thick with anxiety and heat.

"All right." When he shifted weight and took a step back, she added, "But for how long, Grant?"

"What?" He wore an expression of deep confusion.

"How long do you want me to save it?" she asked again, clearly not talking about the half-eaten apple pie on the coffee table any longer.

And by the tension around his mouth, Grant understood. "I wish I could answer that."

"I wish you could, too." She pushed away from the wall and headed into the living room, and to the front door.

He followed her. "See you tomorrow?"

"I don't think so."

"Why not?

She opened the door. "Tomorrow's Caroline's picnic—"

"Right. And you and Jack are going?"

"Yes."

"Well, so am I."

Anna stared at him, confused and frustrated as all hell. He was being incredibly insouciant with her feelings and with her heart. He wanted her now, but he had no clue what the future would bring. She didn't know how long she could do this—have him walk in and out of her life. Have him torture her with his looks, his touch, his moments of domesticity—that she would swear he loved as much as she did.

Oh, things had been so much easier in the beginning, a quick, casual affair with no strings and no falling in love. But lust and great conversation and friendship and care and protectiveness had turned them into something heavier and deeper, and far more fulfilling.

"Well," she said coolly. "I'd better get to packing a killer lunch basket for tomorrow's charity lunch. Lots of competition, and I want to raise as much as I can for Caroline's charity."

That was it. Her attempt at a goodbye. But Grant made no move to leave. His tortured gaze remained on her, as his body remained close. "You gonna make more apple pie?"

She shrugged, tried not to breathe in that clean, woodsy scent of him. "Could be."

He leaned in. His mouth hovered just above hers. He looked beyond frustrated as he glanced up at the door, then back down at her. "I feel like a teenager when I'm with you, Anna."

"I'm not sure what that means."

"It means I want to kiss you all the time, rake my hands up your belly and feel the weight of your breasts in my hands. It means I want to sit up all night and talk with you about everything and nothing. It means I want you to be my first all over again." He huffed out a laugh. "I sound like a fool."

Anna didn't know what to think or feel. She was annoyed at his vacillation, yet she loved his words. They were from his heart, she knew, but they scared her. Why couldn't he understand that what he said drew her closer to him—to a man who might not want her in the end.

He leaned in, close to her ear. "I don't know. I'm so goddamned confused. Back home I knew my life, I knew my routine, I knew I'd never get married. Hell, I knew I'd never meet anyone like…"

He paused, pulled his head back. His eyes filled with unease and lust as he stared at her. It was an odd combination. And a thrilling one.

Anna rose up on her toes and kissed his cheek. "I think you should go now."

"Anna…"

Anna shook her head. She couldn't hear any more. It was pure torture—for both of them. Making love was one thing. It was pleasure with a fabulous escapist quality they both could get lost in for a while, but this was different—this speaking from the heart about fears and desire—it hurt too much.

Knuckles white from gripping the door too hard, Anna muttered a quick, "I'll see ya."

Grant clearly didn't want to leave. He stood there for a moment, perhaps wanting to call upon that selfishness he claimed she brought out in him. But after

a moment, his eyes, once impassioned, turned re-
signed and he nodded. "See you tomorrow, Anna."

And without another word he was gone.

Five

Cool, crisp and heavenly.

It was the perfect description for Louret's new chardonnay, but when Anna stepped out the door of the cottage the following day—Jack in hand—and headed for the main house, she was giving the three-adjective compliment to the lovely November day.

The holidays were approaching, turning the green leaves into brown-and-gold papier mâché, inviting the hot days of Indian summer to take a break and enjoy the winter coolness. Anna loved this time of year. Though she'd passed most holiday time alone, she'd always wished to spend Thanksgiving and Christmas with a family—a big family. And as the climate turned, as the spirit of the season turned, she couldn't help but wonder what this year would bring.

"House, Mama?" Jack asked, squeezing his mother's hand.

"That's right, love."

On the small, well-manicured front lawn of the Vines, under a stand of spectacularly old oak trees, Caroline, her daughters and the staff were hard at work setting tables with linens, flowers and beautifully prepared lunch baskets. With Ashton Winery having hosted a very successful charity auction just one month before, Caroline had been inspired to do a little holiday charity work of her own for the children's shelter.

And she was doing a bang-up job of it.

The Vines looked amazing. The perfect marriage of fall and romance fairly danced in the air, and all about the exterior of the house. The country-style home had earned its nickname with the seemingly endless trail of wild vines growing up its weathered stones and trellises.

And it seemed, Anna mused, that most of Napa Valley's finest had shown up, their pockets full and deep. Everywhere Anna looked she saw people. Guests were milling about, inside the house and out. And on the tables, the numbers of baskets grew by the minute.

At her side Jack squealed. He'd caught sight of Seth and Jillian and little Rachel and took off toward them. When Anna finally caught up with them on the lawn closest to the entrance to the house, Jillian immediately fell into girlfriend mode.

The tall, slender brunette smiled at Anna and touched her shoulder. "Feeling better?"

"Much," Anna said in all sincerity. "Again, thank you so much for watching Jack."

Jillian's smile widened. "Rachel just loves playing with Jack, so if you're ever in need of a babysitter again—or two or three—we'd love it."

"Thanks. That's incredibly generous of you."

"It's no problem at all."

She watched Seth and Jack and Rachel play with two purple beanbags. "Well, I'll definitely let you know, then."

"Sounds good." Jillian shrugged. "Maybe for a night out."

"Sure," she said casually.

"To go on a date or something."

Anna raised a brow. "Or something?"

Jillian shrugged. "Could be a good thing."

Yes, it could be, Anna thought, a tad dispirited. She'd thought about having a night out with Grant too many times to count, but venturing out in public never seemed smart before or after Spencer's death. And now things were slightly strained between them as they tried to figure out where they stood—if they stood.

"How long's it been, Anna?"

Jillian's query tugged her back to reality, and she asked, confused, "How long has it been for what?"

"Since you last had a date?"

Anna went scarlet. "Oh, Lord," she began, keeping her voice down so Seth and anyone else who might be listening wouldn't hear her. "I haven't been on a date in three years.

Jillian looked shocked. "You're kidding."

"I'm afraid not."

Jillian opened her mouth to speak, but nothing came out as a masculine voice said, "What is it you're afraid of, Anna?"

Anna turned. Standing just a few feet away, listening to their private and embarrassing conversation—or hopefully just the tail end of it—was Grant. He looked exceptionally handsome today, as if he was trying to make her lose her mind completely. Faded jeans that molded to his muscular legs—legs that worked the land on a daily basis—and a soft-looking blue shirt, rolled up at the cuffs. His eyes blazed interest and sensuality, and appeared blue-green against his shirt.

Anna didn't waste time blushing. "I…well, I'm afraid that my chocolate chip cookies might be overdone. I left them in the oven just a bit too long." She looked at Jillian, who rolled her lips under her teeth to keep from grinning.

Grant was only watching Anna. "What happened to the apple pie?"

"I decided against it."

"Why's that?"

"Thought I'd try something new."

He stared intently at her. "Something new?"

Once again, they weren't talking about her apple pie.

Grant shrugged, tossed out, "The pie a little too old for your taste? Is that it?"

"No," she said irritably. "Just that the apples seemed a bit sour when I tasted them again." No, this definitely wasn't about pie. "Like they clearly hadn't been ready to be picked."

Grant's brows drew together in a decided frown. He was angry, maybe even a bit confused. But she didn't care. She wanted him to understand that she got it—got him—got that he was in this quasirelationship for the short term and was not ready to be anything more than lovers.

And, heck, if it took talking through apple pie to make him see that—so be it!

Jillian, looking uncomfortable, hustled back over to Seth and the kids.

Grant rubbed his jaw. "You look nice."

"Thanks."

"No, I mean it. Really nice." His gaze swept over her pale pink dress and matching pumps. "Too nice, too damn nice for your own good."

"What's wrong with you today?"

"Nothing," he said gruffly. "So, which basket is yours?"

"Why?"

"You know why, Anna Sheridan. Let's stop playing these silly games." A slow grin tugged at the sides of his mouth. "We're too old for it."

"*We're* too old?" she returned with mock severity.

"Okay. Maybe just me, but isn't this getting ridiculous? We're friends as well as—"

"Stop." She gave a small gasping laugh. It was a lost cause trying to be mad at him, even for something as serious as her future. He was right. They were friends. Probably first and last. She turned around and pointed to the table full of baskets. "That one there."

"Which one *exactly?*" he asked.

"The white wicker with the red bow and the scent of sweet chocolate."

"Thank you," he said, sighing heavily.

"But are you sure you're in the mood for chocolate today, Grant?"

His eyes darkened to a deep forest green and he muttered thickly, "Oh, I'm in the mood."

"Twenty-five dollars isn't going to help the Children's Shelter buy toys for Christmas," Caroline called, continuing to rev up the crowd with her amusing dramatic tone as she waved a wooden gavel from the mock auction block she'd set up. "C'mon, Jared, I have it on good authority that Mercedes has all the fixings for a romantic evening at a remote cabin in that basket."

Before Jared could get a word out, a man from the back of the crowd, who clearly had no idea about Mercedes's condition or her recent marriage, shouted, "I have a remote cabin. One hundred dollars."

"No one bids on my wife," Jared muttered darkly,

his blue eyes hot. "Two hundred and fifty dollars." Jared glanced around. "Any other offers?" he said, as if he were ready to box the next guy who spoke.

No one did.

Caroline cleared her throat and said quickly, "Two fifty going, going, gone."

By Jared's side, Mercedes smiled and hugged him tightly.

"Now, with just a few baskets left," Caroline continued, her hazel eyes dancing. "We're on to this pretty yellow number. It's mine, so my husband had better start—and if he knows what's good for him— end the bidding. What do you say, Lucas?"

From the very front row of the crowd came a loud hoot and a raised hand from the man with the thinning hair and lively blue eyes. "Five hundred dollars."

"Sold!" Caroline shouted before anyone could interject. "To that very handsome gentleman there."

Lucas jumped up and grabbed the basket. Everyone laughed and clapped enthusiastically.

Caroline let them go on for a while, then with a raise of the gavel, she said loudly, "All right then. We're on to this very creative white basket that, if I may say, has an amazing scent of chocolate coming from inside."

Anna held her breath as her basket was brought to the front table. She had this funny feeling in her belly, like sixth-grade gym class and the popularity contest of picking softball teams.

"Twenty-five dollars," a man shouted.

"Fifty dollars," said another.

"Seventy-five."

Anna promptly forgot about gym class and smiled proudly.

"One hundred dollars."

"One twenty-five."

"One thousand dollars."

Anna's hand flew to her throat. The crowd gasped, then began whispering and looking around for who had made such an enormous bid.

"How generous," Caroline said, her own gaze searching the crowd.

No more bids came. In fact, the only sounds that could be heard were coming from nature; wind in the trees, birds, maybe a sneeze or two.

"No other bids?" Caroline said, and with great ceremony added, "All right. One thousand dollars going, going gone."

In those heavy seconds, Anna held perfectly still. She wondered who she would be having lunch with today. She certainly knew who she wanted to have lunch with, but there was no way he could afford...

"Please come up and claim your basket, sir," Caroline said, her gaze still searching the crowd.

Heavy with applause, the crowd parted like the Red Sea. A proud-looking Grant Ashton walked to the front of the podium and reached up for Anna's basket. Anna's mouth dropped open, and didn't close even when Grant thanked Caroline, then walked up to Anna and gestured for her to come with him.

After a quick look at Jillian, who smiled and pointed to an absorbed Rachel and Jack as they played with some building blocks on the grass, Anna followed Grant.

"What have you done?" Anna asked when they finally reached the picnic spot that Caroline and her workers had set up on another pretty expanse of lawn on the east side of the house, complete with blankets and plenty of shade.

"What do you mean, what have I done?" Grant asked as he set the basket down on a pretty blue blanket, then dropped down beside it. "You knew I was going to bid on your basket."

"One thousand dollars, Grant?"

"It's for a good cause."

"But—"

He glanced up, his gaze serious. "I'm no poor farmer, Anna."

She fell silent. She'd obviously made a foolish assumption and was very embarrassed about it.

She gave him a soft smile. "Thank you. And the children thank you."

He returned her smile, took her hand. "Sit with me."

The blue blanket was soft and inviting and she did as he asked. "You know, you've just announced to the entire family that we…well, that we're friends."

Grant chuckled. "As if they didn't know."

True enough. "Well, if you're fine with it, I'm fine with it."

"I'm fine with it," he said succinctly.

She smiled at him and switched gears. "I have to say, I feel an enormous amount of pressure."

"Why's that?"

"You just paid an exorbitant amount of money for some roast chicken, red skinned potato salad, biscuits and a dozen chocolate chip cookies."

"And a piece of that apple pie."

"But—"

He put a hand up. "And I don't care how sour it is."

"All right."

"How about you? Do you care how sour it is?"

With green eyes that made her melt, Anna shook her head. "No, I don't care, either." It wasn't exactly true. She cared. She cared about what happened tomorrow and the next day and the next, but she couldn't resist him, either. Bottom line, she wanted to spend time with him with or without the promise of a future.

Jack came running over, looking hungry. "Eat?"

Anna laughed, and Grant said, "Here you go, Jack. Have some of your mama's roast chicken."

Not far behind, Jillian, Seth and Rachel came walking over. "Sorry to interrupt your picnic," Jillian said. "But Seth has just informed me that—suspiciously—he's not very hungry, so we're going to forgo my basket and head out."

"Your breakfast really filled me up, honey, that's all." Seth had the decency to look sheepish.

Jillian rolled her eyes. "I need to take a cooking class, that's all there is to it. Anyway, before we head inside, Rachel wanted to ask you something."

Anna smiled at the cute little girl. "What is it, sweetie?"

"Can Jack stay at our house tonight?"

"Hmmm. I don't know," Anna said.

Rachel bent her knees, cocked her head and released a very long, "Pleeeeeeease."

Anna laughed. "It's just that he's so little yet, I—"

"I know," Jillian interjected. "We—Seth and I—just thought maybe you could use a night off, for whatever."

Anna stared at her conniving, though very sweet, friend. *For whatever. Right.* This was all about their date discussion earlier.

Grant nudged her. "You know, you could use a night off."

"I had one."

"You were sick." Grant said, picking up a chicken leg. "That's not a night off."

"It'll do you good," Seth added with a smile.

It was a conspiracy. Yet, maybe a good one, a well-deserved one. Anna looked from Seth to Jillian. "Are you sure about this?"

Jillian beamed. "We'd love it."

Anna shrugged. "All right."

Rachel squealed and started listing off all the things she and baby Jack were going to do. Anna could feel Grant's gaze on her.

"We'll bring him home in the morning," Jillian said on a laugh. "Say around, ten?" She looked from Grant to Anna. "Or is that too early?"

Grant chuckled.

Heat surged into Anna's cheeks. "Ten is just fine."

"Now, have a seat," Grant said. "And share this lunch with us. There's plenty of chicken and biscuits."

Seth hunkered down next to Grant and Jack and dug in. "I love biscuits."

Crossing her arms over her chest, Jillian said sternly, "I thought you were full from breakfast?"

Anna laughed as Seth looked up at his wife. "I love you, honey."

She rolled her eyes again and sat down. Anna gave her a biscuit and some potato salad, and the two couples and their children shared lunch and a wonderful afternoon.

Six

It was close to four-thirty when Grant walked Anna back to the cottage. He hadn't left her side since the picnic lunch, and it was a good thing, too, he mused. It hadn't been easy for her to give up Jack for the night. In fact, she'd almost caved at the last minute, and he'd had to remind her how important it was for every parent to take a break—not just sick leave—but a real break every now and then. So, with some gentle prodding from Jillian and a very excited Rachel, Anna had left the Vines looking pretty okay with the whole thing.

Grant watched her swing the empty picnic basket back and forth as she walked to the front door of the cottage. She looked like a child herself, happy, relaxed, unaware of the opulence that surrounded her.

He admired that about her. He was always aware of what was around him, how it affected things, where it would lead him.

He'd like a little of her carefree attitude in times like these.

Anna unlocked the front door, but before she went inside she turned back to him and smiled. "Thanks."

He leaned against the stucco. "For what?"

"For many things, but most of all for giving such a large sum to help the children. That was…"

"It was right. That's all."

She looked at him with true longing in her gaze. In all his years of being a man, from teenager to now, no woman had ever looked at him the way Anna did, as if he was a raw, unchecked, flesh-and-blood man who was really worth something.

"Besides," he said. "I got some pretty delicious cookies out of the deal."

She nodded. "True enough."

On a chuckle, he asked, "So what are your plans for your night off?"

Tossing the basket onto the little side table inside the entryway, Anna said casually, "Watch a movie, read, maybe go to bed early."

"No."

At first, she looked as though she hadn't heard him correctly. Then with a wary smile, she said, "What do you mean, 'no'?"

"A book? Going to bed early? What kind of night off is that?"

She laughed. "Do you have a better suggestion?"

"Yes. I'm taking you out."

A soft pink blush crept up her cheeks. She lifted her chin, tried to look impervious. "Don't you mean you're *asking* me out?"

He shook his head slowly, a grin tugging at his mouth. He couldn't help himself; around her he felt like a damn schoolboy.

"That sounds a little roguish," she said, wrinkling her nose at him. "I have no choice in the matter?"

"Sorry."

"No, you're not."

"No. I'm not."

"All right," she said, trying hard to suppress a smile as she crossed her arms over her spectacular chest. "After you drag me out of this cave by my hair, where are you taking me, Mr. Ashton? Just so I know how to dress."

"Sorry. Can't tell you that."

"But—"

"Be ready at seven-thirty, Miss Sheridan," he said before turning to leave.

"Hey," she called after him.

"What?" He glanced over his shoulder, and Anna rolled her eyes at the devilish grin on his face.

"You forgot to say, 'ugh.'"

"Tiramisu, chocolate gelato and a lovely caramel cheesecake…"

As the waitress listed off the killer dessert menu

at the acclaimed Napa Valley Grill, Anna stared at her date. She couldn't get over it. For a man who always looked deliciously, ruggedly handsome, she'd imagined it was impossible for him to look any better.

She'd been wrong.

Tonight, in a simple crisp white shirt and jeans, he looked downright edible. He'd done something different—not big different, just something. She cocked her head to the side. Maybe it was his short hair that had just a hint of a spike to it, which caused his cheekbones to jut out. Maybe it was the white shirt, made his light tan glow bronze, made his green eyes blaze with the mischievousness of a man half his age.

Whatever it was, she hoped it was going home with her tonight.

"…and pumpkin spice cake," the server finished with a great big smile, as though she were very proud to have remembered all that.

"Sounds wonderful," Anna said, turning to Grant with a brow raised.

Grant nodded. "They all sound great, but we're looking for something a little less fancy, and a little more traditional."

"We have the gelato, like I said." The waitress leaned in, whispered, "It's really just ice cream."

The smile Grant flashed her was so bone-meltingly appealing Anna nearly felt jealous, but after saying a quick, "Thank you," he returned his gaze to Anna. "You don't happen to have a stray piece of apple pie back there, do you?"

There was a tingling in the pit of Anna's stomach as she stared at him, a tingling that had the potential to turn into a very dangerous fire.

"No," said the waitress. "I'm sorry, sir."

"That's all right," Anna said, breaking her gaze with Grant for a moment to acknowledge the young woman. "I think we'll just have the check then."

The girl nodded. "Be right back."

After the waitress had gone, Anna leaned across the table and whispered, "You're becoming obsessed with my apple pie. Do you think that's healthy, Grant?"

His green eyes twinkled. "Maybe not. But addictions are addictions for a reason."

"And what's the reason for this one?"

"Desperation to taste something again and again, but never being fully satisfied. Always wanting more."

A shiver of awareness moved through her, and she felt slightly breathless. "That sounds like a problem indeed."

"Only if the object of your desire is not within reach."

"And you think that someday it might not be?"

"The future is always unsure." His gaze betrayed nothing.

"It can be," she said. "But it doesn't have to be."

She was treading on dangerous ground, and she knew it. They were having a nice, romantic evening and this lazy, sexy way of flirting was moving them into a more serious tone. And she didn't want to go there—not tonight anyway.

The bill came, and Grant quickly paid it, then helped Anna on with her coat and they left the restaurant.

As they were walking to the truck, Anna broke the silence with a nice and easy, "That was a lovely evening. Thank you."

He turned to her, smiled and took her hand. "You're welcome, but it's far from over."

A soft smile tugged at her mouth. "What did you have in mind?"

"Nothing too wild."

"Oh, darn."

He chuckled, opened her door. "Maybe later. But for now, I just want to show you something."

She rolled her eyes at him and grinned. "If I had a nickel for every time I've heard that...."

Under the light of a large yellow moon, the weathered house looked comfortable and familiar. A strange feeling for a man who'd lived in the same place for almost forty years.

Located on a quiet country lane, just a few easy miles from Louret Vineyards, sat a four thousand square foot red farmhouse with white trim on three shaded acres of land. With views of both rolling hills and vineyards, it near took your breath away. And then there were the ancient Douglas firs, oaks and maples that surrounded the home, even followed the woodland path down to the creek, yet willingly steered clear of the run-down, though charming, gazebo near the back of the property.

Grant shut the passenger side door and gave Anna an inquisitive look. "What do you think?"

"Well, I wish I could see it better, but what I can see is wonderful. Needs a bit of work, I think, but it's a beautiful place." She stood at his side, her gaze sprinkled with confusion. "So, why are we here?"

"Just checking things out," was all he felt he wanted to offer at this point, and thankfully she didn't ask anything more—though he felt she wanted to.

Grant took her hand and led her around the side of the house, past a large bay window which was crawling with thick-leafed ivy.

"Is it okay that we're poking around?" Anna asked nervously. "I mean, I know it's for sale, but wouldn't the owners mind us traipsing through their rosemary bushes?"

"There was only one owner and she died six years ago," Grant told her as he guided her up the stone steps and into the forestlike backyard. "She left the house to a friend who died shortly after her. A distant cousin fought for it in court for two years."

"Wow."

Grant snorted derisively. "He doesn't want it, of course. Just wants the money."

"I wonder how long it's been on the market," Anna muttered as they came to a stop just a few feet from a sizable brick patio.

"A little over a year."

He watched Anna glance around from the patio to the built-in brick oven and barbecue. Just a smattering of outdoor lights helped them to see, but the meager illumination only crept out as far as the little vegetable garden ten or so feet from the house.

"What's wrong with it that it's been on the market that long?" Anna asked.

"As you said it needs work. While the owner keeps a gardener on, he's let the house remain in the same condition his cousin left it in. I don't think many people want to take on a job like that—not when they can get a newer home for the same price or less." He shrugged, his gaze moving over the chipped red paint and dusty windows. "It takes the right kind of person to want a piece of land like this, a place a man can lay his hands on, if you know what I mean."

She turned then, looked at him strangely as if she were trying to read his thoughts. "How do you know about the cousin and gardener and how long the house has been on the market and everything?"

"I spoke with the real estate agent."

Confusion lit her eyes once more. "Why?"

"Just curious."

She obviously didn't buy that and said, "I was going to wait until you felt like you wanted to tell me, but I don't think that's going to happen. Why are we really here, Grant?"

Grant pushed a hand through his hair, then shook his head.

"Are you thinking of staying in Napa when this whole mess is resolved?" she continued, undisguised eagerness shining in her beautiful brown eyes.

"No, of course not."

Anna pursed her lips, looking anything but pacified, and Grant felt anything but calm as a quick
and disturbing thought smashed into his brain. He
hadn't been checking out this place just because it reminded him of home, because he felt a little out of
place and homesick in Napa. He'd told himself that
to justify the many visits to this place. No, there was
a part of him that was contemplating staying here, beside this new family that welcomed and intrigued
him, and a woman who made him feel...

Grant inhaled deeply, trying to ease the imagi-
nary vise around his chest. He couldn't be thinking
this way. He had a life, a home in Nebraska with his
kids. And he'd never abandon them like Grace had.
Sure, they were grown with lives of their own, but
they still needed him. And he had vowed long ago
that his own needs would always be second to those
of his kids.

"Grant, what's going on?" she asked gently.

Snapping to attention, Grant said the first thing
that came to his mind. "I've been a little homesick
lately, that's all—and this is the closest thing to a
farm I've seen around here. And well, I wanted to
show you the place, let you see what my home back
in Nebraska was like."

As the cool night air hovered around them, Anna
looked as though she didn't quite believe him, or
maybe she had more questions on her brain. Hell, he
didn't blame her—so did he. Like, why did he really

bring her here? He didn't know himself—at the restaurant he'd had just one thought: *Anna's got to see the house.*

Maybe he'd wanted to share who he was, what he wanted, with her. Who knew?

Refusing to analyze the moment any longer, Grant took her hand again and led her away from the deck and toward a stand of oaks. Hanging between two of the sturdiest trees he'd ever seen was a swing for two, most of its white paint sadly chipped away.

"How about a swing?" he said with a wry grin.

With an uneasy smile of her own, she shrugged. "I'm game if you are. But this thing looks a little unsteady, and I had a pretty big dinner, so don't blame me if we crash to the dirt."

His laughter echoed through the trees. "Looks pretty sturdy to me," he said, sitting down beside her. "See, no worries."

But Grant spoke too soon. The wood made an awful creaking sound, promptly buckled under their weight and dropped an inch or two. Anna gasped. Grant cursed. They both sat very still. After a moment's pause to see if the entire swing would collapse as Anna had predicted, they both turned to look at each other.

Anna bit her lip. "I knew I shouldn't have had that last piece of bread."

They both laughed, and Grant snuck an arm around her. With fingers mentally crossed, they kicked off gently, the moonlight steady as they sailed back and forth.

Grant sighed. "The swing's just the start of it. Like you said, the place needs a lot of work."

"Sure, but isn't that part of the fun?"

"Fun?" he repeated.

"Well, first you see the place and have this instant attraction, right? Then you quickly realize that things aren't as perfect as they seemed on first inspection. So you start planning and wishing and making it into that perfect, magical thing."

In the glow of the moonlight, her eyes sparkled and purred. Grant thought he could stay this way, this close, this comfortable forever. "Are we still talking about the house?"

"We do have a tendency to talk in the abstract," she said, crossing one leg over the other.

Why did her mouth have to look so full and inviting tonight? he wondered madly. Why did she tug at the bottom lip every so often as if she needed to be kissed? Why did she have to wear that red, form-fitting dress tonight? The color made her skin look like satin. Didn't she know how much he wanted her? Didn't she understand how hard it was to keep his hands off of her?

He glanced up at the moon and inhaled the cool air. It did nothing to ease his frustration. "You know what?"

"Hmm?"

"I inherited my grandparents' farm. Didn't have to do much to it. It was pretty comfortable right from the start."

"And you've grown to love it."

"Sure, I have. But the thing is, I've never experienced fixing up a place, calling it my own—that kind of work intrigues me."

She brushed a high-heeled toe up his calf. "You're a man who works with his hands, makes sense."

A shot of heat ripped through him and he brought the swing to a sharp stop.

"What?" she asked, her brows furrowed.

"A man who works with his hands?" he repeated. "Are you trying to kill me here?"

A girlish smile touched her mouth. "I did it again, huh? Can't stay away from double entendres, I guess."

"Looks that way. Just like I can't stay away from you." He pulled her in, kissed her squarely in the mouth.

Being this close to her, breathing in her scent, tasting her, was agony. A kiss would never be enough to satisfy him, never was. He wanted her on the ground, her back to the cool grass, her thighs parted, her eyes a strange mixture of fire and ice as he thrust inside her.

Just the thought had him hard.

His right hand slid behind her neck, his fingers gripped her skull as he changed the angle of his kiss. She followed him as she always did, parting her lips, letting him push his tongue inside and play. With insatiable need guiding him, his free hand drifted down her shoulder to her collarbone and slipped inside her dress.

Anna gasped as his fingers bypassed the lacy cup

of her bra and found her breast. The roar of need inside her blocked out every other sound—even the kicking of her heart. His hand felt so good, so rough, so strong. Her nipples jutted out, urging him to touch, flick, pull.

And he did.

As his mouth moved over hers roughly, insistently, as their tongues warred and their teeth nipped, Grant flicked her nipple between his thumb and forefinger. Anna moaned into his mouth, wanted to crawl on top of him, into his lap and push her hips against his erection.

But something cold and wet landed on her face. At first, in her foggy haze of desire, she thought it was a bug and swatted it away. But then more fat, wet drops pelted her face and head and neck and she jumped back, away from Grant. Her hands went to her cheeks, felt the droplets.

Rain.

And it was coming down hard and fast.

Before she could say a word, Grant snatched her hand and pulled her from the swing. "Hurry," he said, leading her around the house.

They stopped under a short awning, at a side entrance. Anna thought they were going to wait it out there, but when Grant reached into his pocket and took out a key, she realized they were going inside. Thick sheets of misty wet were already making muddy puddles beside the stone pathway, and the air was growing colder by the minute. So was

Anna. In her damp wool dress, she shivered as Grant shoved the key into the lock and opened the door.

"What are we doing?" she asked.

"Getting us out of the rain."

"I know that, but—"

"The car's parked all the way down the driveway."

"But this…they gave you a key to the place?"

"The guy wants to the sell the house pretty badly, okay? So he said to take another look around."

"Another?" she repeated as Grant practically pulled her inside.

"I told you I've been here before."

She didn't understand any of this. Grant's frequent visits to a house he was never going to buy and the fact that he had a key to the place.

Hugging her arms to her chest, Anna followed him into what appeared to be a living room. The large space boasted lovely beamed ceilings with skylights that showed amoebalike shapes of the rain pelting the roof. She traipsed over the rustic brick floors in her sodden heels and sat down on a piece of white-sheet-covered furniture.

She glanced over at Grant. Water dripped from his short dark hair and his blue jeans looked inky-black. He was staring at her, a smile on his face. He broke into a laugh.

"You're all wet," he said.

She grinned, falling into his mood. "So are you."

"It's probably not a good idea…"

"What's that?"

He gave her a devilish glance. "Maybe you should get out of those wet clothes—"

"Oh, my," she drawled.

His grin widened. "Out of those clothes and into a tub."

She sagged dramatically against the back of the couch. "You mean, before I have a relapse?"

He went to her, sat beside her, brought his face close to hers. For a second, Anna couldn't breathe. Grant Ashton did that to her, made her weak and breathless.

With gentle fingers, he brushed aside a strand of wet hair from her cheek. "You shouldn't joke. You've got a kid to look after. You don't want to get sick again."

She sobered slightly. "True. But that means I've got to get back to the cottage to get out of my clothes to take that hot bath. So until the storm lets up a little, I'm afraid—"

"There's always a way, Anna."

His voice was so smooth, so sexy the muscles between her legs contracted. She murmured a breathy, "Huh?"

His fingers moved over her collarbone, slowly. "I know for a fact that the plumbing works in this house."

At first she wasn't sure she'd heard him correctly. He couldn't be suggesting what he was suggesting, right? She sniffed, laughed halfheartedly. "You're crazy."

"No. I'm serious."

And he was. She swallowed hard and tried to slow the slamming of her heart against her ribs. "You've got to be kidding. We can't do that. It's not our house. It would be…"

"It'd be what exactly?"

She just stared at him, every nerve, every muscle in her body tense and ready to spring.

"Crazy? Impulsive?" He raised a brow. "Something our siblings would do?"

"Yes," she said breathlessly. "And we're the responsible ones."

"Maybe just this once we're not."

She stared at him, bit her cheek as waves of excitement, of sensual electricity rolled through her. She'd only done one irresponsible thing in her life and that was her secret affair with Grant. But of course, she'd never regret that.

"A bath you say?"

Grinning, Grant stood up. "Clawfoot and deep."

"Wouldn't a nice hot shower work just as well?"

"Well, sure, but a shower's something you can do on your own."

Heat pummeled her, and her legs were almost shaking. "And I won't be on my own in the bathtub?"

He reached down, pulled her to her feet. "I thought I should be there, but only for a useful purpose."

"And what would that be?"

His hand ran down her sides, pausing as the heels of his palms brushed the sides of her breasts. "Back home, and before people had money, the men—well, a man who was worth his salt at any rate—"

"Which of course you are," she uttered, trembling with longing.

He grinned. "Of course. He'd bring the woman he was caring for pan after pan of hot water, then he'd bathe every inch of her."

Anna pictured him, sitting in the tub, his sun-bronzed chest, heavy with muscle, his arms relaxed on the cool porcelain sides, his mouth and his manhood ready. She closed her eyes and exhaled. "I just want you to know something, Grant. From my heart. You don't have to take me to an abandoned house to seduce me. You don't have to invent reasons to touch me. You don't have to be someone different to make love to me. My arms are open to you always."

Grant closed his eyes for a moment, then opened them and stared down at her. "You slay me, Anna Sheridan." He leaned in and kissed her, soft and tender.

When Anna eased back, she gave over to the grin that pulled at her. "On the other hand, this being bathed thing does sound pretty good."

Laughter erupted in his throat and he pulled her hard against him. "Then let's go, my little vixen."

Seven

Grant passed a hand under the faucet and tested the temperature of the water. Hot. Steam rushed to his face as he heard Anna step into the room.

"How's Jack?" he said without turning around.

"Hey, how did you know I called?"

The sweet familiarity in her voice tugged at his dusty heart. "You're a wonderful mother. Goes with the territory."

She came to stand beside him, put her hand on his shoulder. "Thank you for that."

"Just the truth, Anna." When he did turn, when he looked down into her beautiful face and those large brown eyes, he couldn't help himself. He pulled her to him. "Everybody knows it, and everybody sees how he loves you." His hands settled on her hips. "It's not an easy thing to take on someone else's choices, but the rewards are endless, aren't they?"

"They are." She let her head fall against his chest. "We're kindred spirits, Grant Ashton, you know that?"

He couldn't answer. His throat felt oddly tight. So did his chest. But he knew she was right. God help them both, she was right. "The water's getting too high." He left her for a moment, turned back to the tub and yanked the faucet to the right.

When he returned to her, she was removing her wet dress. Her nipples strained against the white, wet fabric of her bra, just as Grant strained against the fly of his jeans. His gaze moved over every inch of her, from her long neck to the weight of her breasts, to her flat stomach to the curve of her hips, to her slender legs and tiny feet.

"You'd better get in the water," Grant muttered, sweat breaking out on his forehead, "before I go in search of a condom."

She smiled and unhooked her bra, let it fall to the floor. "Don't you mean we'd better get in the water?"

"Sorry?" He hadn't heard her. Not through the hazy red glow of full breasts and hard pink nipples.

"Didn't you think I'd take you seriously when you suggested a bath for two?"

"Hell no," he replied.

"So that was just a ploy to get me naked?"

"Hell yes!" he said with a grin.

Unable to stop herself, Anna closed in on him and

started with the buttons on his shirt. "You're taking a bath with me, farm boy." She laughed at his raised brow. "And I'm taking your clothes off."

For Anna it was a sure treat to strip this man bare. She'd thought about it from the moment he'd picked her up tonight. Flicking off button after button, pulling back the flaps of white cotton, hauling them over his powerful shoulders and down his muscular arms until he was bare from head to hips.

Then she took a tiny step back to admire him.

This was no puny, pale executive who sat behind a desk all day and never got his finely manicured fingernails dirty—no, this was a man who worked outdoors, worked with his hands, worked up a sweat as he pushed his body to the limit.

With her heart in her throat, she ran her hands down his chest. Tan, ripped and smooth, with just the perfect amount of hair. Before she did something crazy and far too erotic for a schoolteacher to even be thinking about—like, digging her nails into his chest while grinding her hips against the erection she felt pressing against her belly—she let her fingers drift downward, down to the waistband of his jeans.

"Need some help?" he asked, his tone raw with unmasked desire.

"No, I think I've got everything under control." It was a lie. As she loosened his belt, unzipped his fly and yanked down both his jeans and boxers, she felt anything but controlled.

"I took the being bathed part seriously, you know,"

she told him as she stepped into the bathtub, the hot water assaulting her skin as she sat down.

Grant followed, sat opposite her. "But there's no soap."

"We could pretend."

He grinned, leaned toward her and started rubbing his hands together, as though he were gathering a mock lather. Leaning back in the tub, Anna waited, her heart thumping with anticipation. This was such complete madness. This whole thing. Where they were, what they were doing—and all as the rain pounded the roof like sodden bullets.

He started with her toes, massaging them long and slow until she released the breath she'd been holding. Up to her ankles and calves.

The hot water acted like a tonic, making her a little light-headed.

Up to her knees and thighs. First her outer thighs, then he shifted. He kneaded the flesh of her inner thighs, raking up, up until he was poised at the soft, swollen folds at her center. She sucked air between her teeth, wondering, hoping he would delve further, let his fingers part her, burrow deep and find the opening to her body. But he was hell-bent on teasing her before giving her the pleasure of release.

His strokes were slow and strong. So many times he came close to her. So many times he played, in her hair, with the concave and highly sensitive skin just below her buttocks.

Anna fairly burned with desire. She uttered a faint,

"Please…" and thrust her hips up, trying to urge his fingers to do more than play.

Grant's hot gaze traveled from her swollen breasts to her swollen labia just inches below the water. "I suppose you need to be washed everywhere."

"Yes," she muttered hoarsely.

"All right, sweetheart. Spread your legs for me."

Anna gasped, her core throbbing as she opened her legs wide.

"Yes," he said on a groan. "You are so beautiful, Anna."

Her mouth was like cotton, her skin tingled as she waited. Then, finally, she felt him, felt him play with her woman's hair, then slip his middle finger between her folds, searching and finding the entrance to her body. She cried out, let her head drop to one side as he entered her. Grant made her feel heavy and light and desperate. He knew what he was doing, no amateur when it came to a woman's body. With expert precision, he caressed the swollen bud at her core as he flicked his middle finger deep inside her.

Anna opened her legs wider. "No more," she managed.

"What?"

"No more of this. I want you." She searched the water wildly, found him and fisted his erection. "I want this inside me."

Finding a new energy as her body twisted and turned inside her hot skin, Anna rose up, pushed Grant back against the white porcelain and straddled him.

As the steam rose around them, Anna positioned herself over his erection and promptly sat down. She gasped as his hot, hard thickness filled her. Groaning, Grant thrust his hips upward. His hands found her hips and his fingers dug into her flesh as he hauled her back and forth. The movement was jarring and wonderful and Anna could hardly breathe.

Water splashed over the sides of the tub, but neither one of them noticed. Grant grabbed for her breasts, tugged and flicked at her nipples as she rode him. Sensation pounded in her blood. Her skin was hot, prickly and her womb ached and begged for release.

Grant didn't waver. As she rose and dropped back against him, his fingers worked her nipples until she was beyond frustration. Pulsing heat grew and grew and she writhed and wriggled and smashed her hips against him. Then suddenly, from deep down, overwhelming spasms erupted. Sweat trickled down her face to her neck. She moaned over and over and over, and heard Grant curse, felt him grow impossibly harder inside her, then hot wetness spread through her core.

She dropped to his chest, her breathing labored, her gaze hazy, her hair as wet as her skin.

Grant wrapped his arms around her, kissed her neck and whispered in her ear, "I'm sorry, Anna."

It took her a moment to hear him, understand him. "For what?"

"No protection."

"It's okay," she said softly. He didn't know how

okay, she thought as aftershocks moved through her sensitive body.

"No, I should've—"

"Stop, please." The moment was lovely and delicious and she didn't want to go where they were headed. But Grant was quiet and she could fairly feel him ruminating over what he thought he had allowed to happen. "Listen," she sat up slightly, her mouth close to his. She kissed him and uttered against his lips, "It wouldn't have mattered if you had worn something—"

"Of course it matters. We just talked about this and then I tossed all sense out of the window...." He cursed. "It's you." He nuzzled her mouth with his, nipped at her lower lip with his teeth. "You make me mad, weak and completely desperate. I want you every damn second of every damn day."

"Grant."

"What?"

Her hands went to his face. She took a breath and just told him the truth. "I can't get pregnant."

He took a moment to answer. "What?"

"I have endometriosis. The doctors say it's virtually impossible."

"Oh, God." Grant's arms tightened around her, his eyes filled with concern. "Anna, I'm so sorry."

"It's okay. I have Jack now..."

"Why didn't you tell me before?"

"I don't know."

She did know. But how could she look at this man

she loved and tell him she was embarrassed, tell him that sometimes she didn't feel like a whole woman?

Grant placed a hand to the back of her head and gently pulled her down to lay on his chest once more. There was no more to say. He was still connected to her, and she felt protected and cherished as he stroked her back in slow, easy circles, and as the water slowly cooled around them.

When the rain let up an hour later, Grant and Anna grabbed their chance and hustled down to the car. The ride home was quiet, and Anna wondered if her admission had changed Grant's feelings for her or made him uncomfortable in any way. But after a moment, he reached out and covered her hand with his. He held on to her all the way up the Louret Vineyard drive and as they walked the short distance from his truck to the door of her cottage.

"I had a great time tonight," she said, her back to the open cottage door.

Grant folded his arms over his chest. "Not going to invite me in?"

A smile broke on her face. "Well, I suppose. Would you like to watch a movie or something?"

"Or something?" He stared at her intently.

"We could play Monopoly?"

"How about a sleepover?"

Her brows shot up. "But I don't think I have a sleeping bag."

"I'm staying all night," he muttered tersely, "And

I'm staying in your bed." He picked her up and tossed her over his shoulder like she weighed little more than a sack of feed and stalked inside the cottage.

She was laughing almost to the point of tears when he entered her bedroom and dropped her onto the bed. But she quickly sobered as he started to peel off her clothes, then his own.

"I suppose my clothes were still a little wet," she said breathlessly as he gently rolled her onto her belly.

"They aren't the only thing," Grant murmured.

Her breath hitched as every muscle, every nerve went on alert. "And everyone thinks you're such a good, down-home boy, Grant Ashton. But you're not."

"No. I'm not."

Excitement raced through her blood as she felt the delicious weight of his body on her, his chest hair tickling her back, his erection hard and ready against her buttocks.

His lips moved close to her ear, and she felt his tongue, felt just a slip of wet brush her inner ear. She moaned hungrily, wriggled beneath him hoping to entice him into her body where he belonged.

"Tell me what you want, Anna," he uttered, his voice tight with restraint.

"You. Just you."

He groaned. "You always have me." He nudged her thighs apart with his thigh, eased his erection into her just an inch, then gripped her shoulders and sank deep into her core.

Anna could barely catch her breath, barely think.

But instinct had her moving, had her following Grant as he pumped inside her, as he kissed her neck, his teeth grazing her skin. His hand left her shoulder and slipped downward, through her wet curls and to the aching center of her. Anna sucked air through her teeth as her nipples stiffened in response.

Slow and steady, he worked her, his thrusts making her wet, his caresses making her moan.

It didn't take long for the response Grant wanted. Anna's legs began to tremble, her skin went hot and prickly, and she cried out, came apart in his hand.

But even through her climax she pumped her hips back, and soon it was Grant whose breathing changed.

"What are we going to do about this?" he whispered in her ear.

"About what?" she uttered into the pillow.

"This. Us. You and me." He thrust into her, hard and wonderful.

"Grant…"

But Grant was gone, flying. He called out, guttural, almost angry, bucking and sinking his fingers into her flesh. Finally he collapsed on top of her. His hands burrowed under her and held her tightly, as he kissed her back, nuzzled her skin.

"You are so amazing," he said with a strange strain of melancholy to his tone.

She hugged his arms, loved the weight of his body on top of hers. "It's just the afterglow talking."

"No, it's the truth. You make me weak, Anna. Like the day I found out Ford and Abigail were mine.

Weak, and yet so powerful. And happy." He buried his face in her neck. "Doesn't make any sense, does it?"

"Yes, it does." Weakness was a disease they'd both caught. She'd just decided to give in to it.

"What are we going to do?" he said again, sounding soul weary.

"Not we, Grant," she said gently. "You. It's more than obvious where my heart is, who my heart belongs to. It's scary, I know, but I won't deny my feelings for you or what I want for us."

Grant said nothing. He rolled them both to the side so they were spooning. For a moment, Anna thought to say something more, but she knew what she wanted to hear from him was nothing that could be forced. Time would tell.

They fell asleep that way, her back to his chest, arms wrapped, feet entwined.

The next morning they awoke with a start to the sound of insistent knocking on the front door.

Groggily Anna looked up and glanced at the clock. "Seven-thirty."

From behind her, Grant muttered a hoarse, "It's probably Seth and Jillian bringing Jack back."

"This early?"

"Maybe he missed you."

Panic sank into Anna's bones and she leaped up, jumped off the bed and grabbed for her robe. Maybe something had happened. Oh, God, she'd never forgive herself if something…

No, she couldn't even go there.

Grant was right behind her as she practically flew to the cottage door and hauled it back madly.

But there was no little boy with bright green eyes, calling, "Mama, Mama, Mama," on the small porch. Lucas and Caroline stood there, their faces drawn and worried.

Caroline spoke first. "Sorry, Grant, Anna."

"Is something wrong?" Anna asked quickly and without care regarding her and Grant's mussed hair and skimpy attire. Clearly their affair was out in the open now. "Is it Jack?"

Lucas shook his head. "No, Jack's fine. Having breakfast with Rachel and Seth."

"We've come at a bad time," Caroline said, trying not to look directly into the cottage in case she should see something from their late-night tryst.

"I'm afraid there's no good time for this," Lucas said, his blue eyes uneasy and focused on Grant. "Can you come up to the house?"

Grant stiffened. "Right now?"

"Yeah."

"All right."

Without thought, Anna stepped slightly in front of him, and asked Lucas, "Why does he need to come up to the house?"

Caroline met Grant's gaze and frowned. "The police are waiting. They want to speak with you."

Eight

"I'm going with you."

Forgetting for a moment that Caroline and Lucas still remained waiting at the front door, Grant shook his head at Anna. "No."

Her hands went to her hips. "What do you mean, no?"

"If this is going to happen all over again, I don't want you there with me."

An angry blush stained her cheeks, and the sight frustrated the hell out of Grant. Just hours ago, he'd caused a pretty pink glow to surface on her pale skin, but for an entirely different reason.

He turned to Caroline and Lucas. "Could you excuse us for a second?"

"Of course," they said in unison.

Grant hardly waited for the response. He had Anna's hand and was tugging her into the bedroom. Sunshine poured through the window and almost blinded him as he walked through the door. With a sigh, he sat her down on the rumpled bed, then started to pace. "Look, I know where your mind is going with this, and it's not some kind of rejection—"

"Sounds like it to me."

"Well, it's not."

"Then what is it?" she demanded, her gaze following him as he walked, as his jaw worked.

"What is it, Grant?" she repeated. "More protection? Like the last time? Because Jack and I don't need it anymore."

"Yes, you do."

"Spencer is gone, and I've had no threats, no reporters."

"If the threat is gone then why are you still in Napa?" Grant asked darkly.

Her face went slightly pale, and she chewed the inside of her lip. "Until the murder is solved I thought it would be best—"

"See," Grant interrupted, "you think there's still something to be concerned about."

"I should be there with you, dammit."

"No."

"Stop moving for a minute." When he did, she shook her head helplessly. "I don't understand you."

The stirring of emotions in his gut had him feeling queasy. He'd lived a casual, calm life. He wasn't prepared for this soap opera type of existence, this up and down, unsure, one revelation after the other feeling. He walked over to her and sank to his knees at her feet. "All right." With his eyes locked on hers, he placed his hands on either side of the bed, imprisoning her. "You know, I'll always protect you and Jack—" he looked at the ceiling, released a heavy breath "—but that's not what my objection to your coming with me is all about."

Her large brown eyes implored him. "What is it then?"

His voice dropped, sounded hoarse. "I'm ashamed, Anna. Ashamed of my suspect status, of my out of control life. I'm ashamed of having you see me as less of a…" He shook his head.

Her hands cupped his face. "C'mon, Grant. I know the truth here. I know where you were that night. There's nothing for you to feel—"

"I've got to go." He pushed to his feet.

"Wait—"

"That bastard Ryland's waiting for me, Anna, and he'll think I'm hiding something if I take too long."

She stayed where she was, on the bed with its messy sheets and the imprints of their heads on the pillows.

"I'll be back," he said gently, silently asking her to let him go.

Her jaw looked tight, her eyes unsure, but she finally nodded. "All right."

He was almost out the door when he turned, stalked back to her and pulled her into his arms. His gaze searched hers. "Dammit, Anna. You know how much I need you."

Tilting his head, he kissed her hard on the mouth. When he came up for air, he saw what he needed to see.

Her eyes were bright and supportive, and though her smile was a little tremulous, it was there. "Go," she said.

It wasn't easy on all accounts, but he did.

When Grant entered the library with Lucas and Caroline he wasn't surprised to find Detective Ryland standing with his back to the window, his dark brown hair slicked back, his eyes narrowed as if he half expected a crime to be taking place right then and there. Grant had always felt as though Ryland had a personal vendetta against him, or maybe he just truly believed Grant had murdered his own father in cold blood and desperately wanted to put him away for life.

Grant's gaze shifted to the man sitting on the couch with a pensive look. Edgar Kent, the criminal lawyer Caroline had hired for his defense, stood up when he saw his former client and offered him a weak smile. "Hello there, Grant."

A ball of stress rolled good and hard through Grant's gut. Was he actually going to need his lawyer again? Had Caroline called Kent? Did she know more about this meeting than she'd let on during the walk over here?

Well, whatever way this mess went, Grant wasn't about to fold, to cave under the pressure. It wasn't in his nature to give in. On sturdy legs, he walked over to Kent and shook his hand, but after what Ryland had put him through over the past several months, Grant had no pleasantries for the man and only acknowledged him with a raise of the chin.

Ryland didn't seem to care. His muddy gaze remained fixed on Grant and he looked agitated, one hand in his pocket, and by the sound of the jingling, fiddling with the keys to his sedan.

"No Detective Holbrook today?" Grant asked, speaking about the strongly built, blue-eyed female detective who was usually attached to Ryland's hip.

Ryland shook his head. "My partner is following a very interesting lead in this case. Didn't want to tear her away. Besides," he said with a tight grin, "I can handle this myself."

"Can I get you something to drink, Grant?" Caroline asked him quickly, her eyes warm, but her voice a little too anxious.

"No, thanks, Caroline." He eyeballed Ryland. "I'd just like to know why I'm here."

Ryland made a move to speak, but Edgar Kent held up a hand. "Grant, there's been some new information that's come to light—"

"New information?" Grant repeated. "Like what? More on the blackmailer? Do you know who it is? What about the sketch?"

His own agitation, his desperation to get to the

bottom of the mystery, to solve this crime and return to his normal life, jarred him.

Edgar motioned to the chair beside him. "Have a seat, Grant."

"I'd rather stand."

Ryland snorted, and as usual cut through the preliminaries and got to business. It was actually the one trait Grant respected in the man. "Enough of this. Look, Ashton, I want to know something—and I want the truth."

"Whether you believe it or not, that's all I've ever given you," Grant muttered through gritted teeth.

Ryland snorted again. "Does the name Sally Simple mean anything to you?"

The question took a moment to register in Grant's brain. All he heard for a moment was buzzing, a deafening buzz that made him want to shove his hands over his ears. But then, the words formed again and made sense. Shock slammed into him, and he asked the detective hoarsely, "What did you say?"

"Sally Simple," Ryland repeated, looking as though his patience was wearing thin. "I asked if the name meant anything to you, but by the look on your face—" he moved closer "—I can see that it does."

Years rolled back like a cosmic carpet, and Grant saw his mother's face, kind and loving. He saw his hometown, the lawn he used to play on at school and train tracks he and his friends used to sit beside to talk about girls and cars and an unsure future. He saw his grandparents and their strict, though gentle spirits. These were the people and places that he'd attached himself to, and their presence and their memory had carried him through many a tough time.

And they would again, it seemed.

"Grant," Edgar began, sitting forward in his seat. "Maybe we should talk privately?"

Grant knifed a hand through his hair. "I don't understand."

Edgar looked at Lucas, then Caroline. "Is there somewhere we could go?"

"Of course," Caroline said.

"Caroline's garden is plenty private," Lucas said, his arm curling around his wife's waist as if to protect her from any more shock and pain that might be coming from this new development.

His hand still in his pocket, those damn keys jingling almost merrily, Ryland said, "More to hide, Ashton?"

But Grant wasn't listening to any of them. His chest was tight and his mind reeled with confusion. "Why do you want to know about Sally Simple?" he asked Ryland.

"Oh, no, no." Ryland shook his head slowly. "That's not the way this is going to go. You tell us and we tell you. In that order."

Grant's lips thinned.

Ryland shrugged. "While Mr. Ashton speaks with his attorney, maybe I should head down to your cottage," Ryland said to Caroline. "Ask Miss Sheridan a few questions?"

"You're an ass, Ryland," Grant muttered.

The detective's brows shot up. "Better watch yourself, Ashton, or you'll find yourself back in that cell before nightfall, shackled and eating that gray stew you seemed to like so much."

"On what charge?" Grant snarled. "Telling the truth to an officer?"

"I said, watch it."

Grant had never been so angry in his life, and he didn't give a damn who he insulted. "You don't go near her. She has nothing to do with this, and you know it!"

Ryland walked over to Grant and stood directly in front of him. He was a good four inches shorter than Grant, but the thick muscles of his character made up for it. The two men stared at each other.

"Understand this, Mr. Ashton," Ryland said slowly, deliberately. "I will get to the truth of this matter one way or another."

"No matter who gets in the way, right?" Grant spat out.

With a quick laugh, Ryland said, "Now, you're making me sound like…well, like Spencer Ashton."

"All right, that's enough," Edgar Kent said testily, springing out of his seat.

"Sit back down, Edgar," Grant said, having about enough of this conversation and attempts at intimidation. "Ryland, you, too. Anna has no idea who Sally Simple is."

Perhaps noting that Grant was about to spill the

beans, Ryland backed off. "But you do?" he said, sitting on the arm of a leather chair.

Protecting a woman who had always been there for him from the day they'd met, protecting his two grown kids and a little boy he'd just begun to love with all his heart, protecting a family who was generous and kind, and God help him, protecting himself and a possible future?

Or protecting a woman who had rejected every kindness he and his family had offered her, a woman who had run out on her babies when they'd needed her most.

It should've been an easy choice, but it wasn't.

Nausea hit him full-on, but he gritted his teeth. "Sally Simple is a doll."

It was as if a bomb of silence had been tossed into the room. Caroline looked at Lucas, and Lucas back at her. Edgar stared off into space, a tight, pinched expression on his face. And Ryland? Ryland looked straight at him.

Grant scrubbed a hand over his stubbled jaw and continued, "After my mother died and my grandparents took responsibility for us, things really changed. Where I accepted my situation, embraced my grandparents and my new life, Grace—my sister—became detached, angry, even violent at times. My grandmother really tried to get through to her, spent a lot of time cooking, gardening, shopping with her— gave her anything she wanted. She even made her a doll for Christmas that year. Ten times more beautiful than any store-bought doll, and Grace took to her immediately. She named her Sally. Sally for our mother and Simple for the life she thought she'd always lead in Nebraska." As Grant spoke, the anger and resentment he had toward his sister for rejecting the only family he'd had, for making it tougher at home, making it so much harder for him to let go of his mother's memory, came back full force. "And though she kept close to that doll, she grew even further away from all of us. Later on, that doll moved aside for man after man after man. Until eventually she left us all together for what I can only assume was the biggest loser in the bunch."

A strange cloud of misery hovered in Grant's chest. He hadn't dealt with his feelings for his sister and all that she'd done to him and to her children. No, he hadn't had the time to deal with it. Whenever the memories of those days had assaulted him, he'd pushed them back, pushed them aside, looked at his kids and forced himself to move forward for them and for his own sanity.

Not surprisingly, it was Ryland who broke the thick silence in the room. "When was the last time you saw your sister, Mr. Ashton?"

The sudden thread of respect in the detective's voice pulled Grant back to reality. "The day before she ran off with some guy, some traveling salesman, and left her two children."

"Which you raised, is that right?"

Grant eyed the man who'd been the knife in his wound for months now. "That's right."

"And you haven't heard from her since?"

"No. I hardly wanted to after all she'd done, and I thought it would be worse for the kids as time went on."

"Why's that?" Ryland asked.

"She was more of Spencer's twin than mine, and that, as you know, wouldn't have made her a very good mother."

"And you never met this man she ran off with? This salesman?"

"No. Grace always sneaked around. You never knew who she was…with—" Grant exhaled heavily "—at any given time. Never met any salesman."

Nodding thoughtfully, Ryland finally looked away, looked down to his notepad and began to scribble.

"Now, it's my turn, Detective," Grant said tightly. "Why exactly are you asking about that doll? And how'd you get the name?"

Ryland glanced up from his notes. He looked unsure, as though he were contemplating going back on his word and not letting Grant in on the information he had about Sally Simple. Then he gave a quick sniff, reached into his pocket and handed Grant a piece of paper.

Grant studied the slip of paper. It seemed to be a bank statement. On closer inspection, he saw the name on the account. His pulse stirred and an icy fear crept through him. He looked up.

Ryland didn't need a query to give an answer. "We believe that Grace and her husband have been the ones blackmailing Spencer for the past ten years."

Behind Grant, Edgar cursed, and Caroline sucked in a breath. "You really think that Grant's sister is the blackmailer?"

Lucas practically barked, "What?"

Grant just shook his head, fear and anger knotting inside him at the idea that his own blood would stoop so low. Then again, he realized, Grace had Spencer's blood running through her veins, too. "But why would she? How would she? She didn't even know Spencer."

"She knew him," Ryland assured Grant. "And obviously wasn't too happy about him running out on you and your mother when you were kids. She needed the money and he needed her to stay silent."

"Silent?"

"That's right. If the word got out that he'd never divorced your mother, things would've gotten tricky for him."

"But the word did get out," Grant said.

"Yes. And a short time later Spencer was murdered."

"But why?" Caroline asked.

Ryland stood up. "We believe, when Spencer found out that Grant was in Napa, he stopped paying Grace—that's when the money stopped rolling in to the Sally Simple account. No doubt Spencer realized that everyone would know the truth soon enough."

A slow, sickening feeling moved through Grant. "You think Grace killed Spencer?"

"We think her husband was the one who actually pulled the trigger, but she was definitely an accessory."

"Oh, Grant," Caroline whispered, placing her hand on his shoulder.

Grant moved away. He felt numb and sick, and he just couldn't have anyone touching him. He felt strangely dirty. First Spencer, now Grace—totally and completely corrupt.

Where the hell had he come from?

His eyes narrowed as he looked at the detective. "Why all this, Ryland? Calling me up here, with my lawyer, making me believe—"

"Listen, Ashton," Ryland began, his tone lacking in argument for once. "I wasn't a hundred percent convinced you had nothing to do with this. I had to see if you would give me the information on Sally Simple or hide it. I had to see your reaction to know for sure."

"And now?" asked Edgar Kent.

"Yeah. And now?" Grant asked tightly.

Ryland lifted a hand in the air. "Now you're free to head back to Nebraska if that's what you'd like."

"Just like that?" Grant said.

"Just like that."

As Grant stood there half empty inside, half sickened by what he'd just heard, and by the horrifying news that he was going to have to give to Ford and a very pregnant Abigail, Ryland shook Lucas's hand, then Caroline's and finally walked over to Grant.

The man was not one for apologies, even if one was warranted, but he did offer his hand. It wasn't easy for Grant to take the detective's bit of peace.

After all, the man had treated him like a cold, hard criminal. But Grant wasn't going to return home feeling any more pissed off than he did, any more jaded than he already did. He'd make peace with this part of his journey and move on with it.

After he shook Ryland's hand, the detective gave them all a wave and headed for the door. But Grant called him back tiredly, "Detective?"

Ryland turned. "Yes?"

"Do you know where Grace is?"

"We do."

"Will you let me know when she's in custody?"

Ryland hesitated for a moment, then nodded. "Sure."

Grant felt as though his head was about to explode as he stalked down the stone steps toward the carriage house. He wasn't going anywhere near the cottage today. He was ashamed and sickened by what he'd just heard, and he wasn't about to show his face to the woman that loved him. He wanted to crawl into a hole for a good week and forget the past few months ever happened.

His sister was wanted for the murder of their father.

It was almost too much to bear. Grant felt guilty as hell. Maybe he should've sought her out, loved her more as a child, helped her to deal with their mother's death, helped her to see the right path.

But hadn't he tried that so many times? And hadn't he failed just as many times?

When he reached his front door, he didn't go in. He dropped on the porch steps and put his head in his hands.

A cool breeze kicked up around him, made him feel colder and more alone than he had in that tiny, rank San Francisco jail cell. He wanted to call Ford and Abigail right now, wanted to lean on them for once, but he knew that wasn't a good idea. Not yet, anyway. Abigail was in a delicate condition and he didn't want to upset her. And Ford would want answers, and if Grant didn't supply them immediately Grant knew Ford would catch the first plane out of here to get them himself. And Ford needed to be there for his sister—it was hard enough that Grant hadn't been able to go to his daughter. No, Grant thought, he had to wait, wait until he'd seen Grace face-to-face and gotten the whole story.

A dark laugh escaped his throat. If Grace would even offer the truth at this point.

"Can I join you?"

Grant glanced up, up into the beautiful brown eyes of an angel. Dressed in a white sweater and tan pants, Anna's hair fell soft around her face, she looked pure and sweet, and he thought he'd be doing her a great disservice by having her sit beside him—beside a man with such hate, such disgust and contempt running through his blood.

His fingers scraped against the aging wood of the porch as his hands balled into fists. He hated how his heart tugged, hated how his breathing calmed when

Anna was around. He wanted to grab her and pull her into his arms, make her sit on his lap and touch his face.

He was a fool.

Realizing she wasn't going to get an invitation, Anna sat beside him anyway. "I went up to the house after you."

Ashamed, but not angry, Grant nodded. "So you know what happened then."

"No. All I know, all I wanted to know, is that you're okay and you're still here."

"That's right. They won't be taking me to jail this time around."

She flinched at the bitterness in his tone. "I'd intended to listen in, help you if you needed me, *be there* if you needed me, regardless of what you said, but—"

"But?"

She took his cold hand, held it steady in her warm one. "I realized I can't push myself on you or your life. No matter how much I want to."

He turned to her. "Anna, you don't push—"

"So I went to see Jack instead," she said quickly, obviously not wanting to delve into a discussion that never seemed to go any further than her desires for the future.

"Where is Jack?" Grant asked.

"Still with Rachel and Seth and Jillian."

"Playing?"

"They were headed to the lake today. And he was so excited to see the frogs and ducks, I didn't want to steal him away from that."

But this time, Grant didn't let her leave the future or her feelings on the roadside of their affair. He wanted—no, he *needed* to hear how she felt. He was selfish and masochistic, but right now, after months and months of suspicion and then today's dump of information, he wanted to hear that someone cared. "Was there any other reason you let Jack stay and play at the Vines today?"

She heaved a sigh, smiled. "As always, Grant, I'm here for you if you need me. And I thought you might. I'm here if you need me and if you want me— no pressure, no demands."

"Why?"

"Because I love you, you idiot."

He chuckled halfheartedly as the words—the three sweet ones—wrapped around him, made him feel as if he could breathe again, made him feel protected and stable. She'd given him so much and he continually asked for more. All knowing full well he would hurt her in the end.

Was he no better than his sister?

Was he no better than his father?

His heart pumping wildly in his blood, he stood up and offered her a hand. "I want to take you to bed."

Without a word, Anna slid her fingers to his palm, stood up beside him and let him guide her into the house.

Nine

"**I** want to go slow. Really slow."

"Okay." Her shirt and jeans strewn over the chair in the corner of the bedroom, Anna smiled at Grant as she lay back against the cool white sheets and beckoned for him to come to her. Being nude before him no longer held the shades of embarrassment it once did. Over the past few months, she had shared her heart, let him see the deepest caverns of her feelings and given in to her desires—and all of that had freed her in so many ways.

"I want to forget everything that I heard today," Grant said, inching over her from toe to knee to hip, belly, breasts and lips until he hovered above her, naked and hard.

She held his gaze. "Grant…"

"Just for today," he said with obvious desperation. "Hell, just for a few hours."

Anna let her hands travel over his chest, feeling every muscle, every indentation. It was strange and oddly erotic how lean his skin was, how the thickness of his muscles stretched and bunched underneath. Swallowing her desire, she played with his nipple, circling the hard bud lazily, then rolling it between her fingers.

His voice was rough, his breathing a little unsteady as he muttered, "You'll let me forget then, Anna?"

"Yes," she said on a sigh. "Let's both forget."

"What do you want to forget, sweetheart?" he asked, his tone hoarse with desire.

"That if this case is over, we're both going home," she uttered as she bent her head and touched his nipple with her tongue.

Grant sucked in a breath, then grasped her head with his hand and forced her mouth to his. It was a crushing kiss—nothing slow and easy about it. All consuming and desperate, as if he couldn't hear anything more, didn't want to hear anything more. His tongue urged her lips apart as he raked his thumb across her nipple. She jumped slightly, the muscles in her womb contracting as wet heat leaked from the opening to her body.

As he nipped and nuzzled her mouth, his hand moved down her torso, down over her belly and cupped her. Need hummed throughout her body, and she squirmed and moaned, her hips thrusting upward, begging him to play, begging him to put her out of her misery so she could start over, go slowly and decadently the second time around.

A very male laugh, a proud growling laugh escaped his throat as he left her mouth and moved his body down, scraped his hot skin over her breasts and belly.

His tongue traced the path, lapping at her navel, her hipbones, his own flesh scented with pure male and salty sweat. A swirling bundle of heat sang in her core as she waited, breathing heavily, wriggling uncontrollably beneath him.

At first, his fingers gently slid between the curls at her center, nudging each fold aside as he searched for her swollen cleft. Anna gasped, her hands wild as she clumsily grasped for his hair.

"I want to stay here for at least an hour," Grant said, the urgent beats of his breath stealing over her thighs. "I want you to cry out against my mouth over and over, then we'll start again in any position you want."

"Just one position?" she whispered, her legs tingling with anticipation.

"God, I hope not."

Her womb felt heavy and tight and ready, and just when Anna wondered if she could make it another second without his touch, Grant thrust her thighs open and dipped his head.

Anna cried out, tilting her hips up as he fed on her hot flesh, his tongue sliding past the thick curls to the place where she ached.

The bed seemed too small suddenly, the earth seemed unsteady as he flicked and tugged at her sex. Tension surged through her womb, coiling, contracting. She stiffened, words and sounds of desire caught in her throat as the rush of climax thundered through her body.

Grant nuzzled her, softly taking her contractions into his mouth.

"Grant, please," she uttered, after finding her voice. "Please."

She didn't need any more than that. Understanding exactly what she wanted, Grant gave her wet flesh one last kiss before sitting up. With one hand under her buttocks, he lifted her hips and positioned himself above her, his erection long and so hard she could feel the tip pulsing against her thigh.

"Maybe we should have some protection," Anna said softly.

Grant shook his head, looked pained with need. "We don't need the barriers."

"There's still a chance, Grant. It's a very small one, but…"

"No."

"Grant…"

"Just you and me. Nothing else." His eyes went a strange shade of inky-green and he lowered himself to her, until the hard tip of his erection jutted up against the soft, wet cove of her body.

Anna couldn't think, couldn't try to reason with herself or with him. Her mind was a blurry shade of violet, and her legs began to tremble with anticipation. It was like this every time they were together—wondering how he would feel, wondering how she would stretch to accommodate him, hoping he would find forgiveness and love with each thrust inside her.

Feeling suddenly urgent, Anna lifted her hips, causing his erection to slide a few inches into her body. Grant sucked air through his teeth and shuddered. He pushed into her, all the way, until they joined, hip to hip. There, he paused, his mouth to hers, his chest to hers.

He kissed her softly, then began to move. His thrusts were exquisite torture, and Anna couldn't help herself, she reached around his waist and placed her hands on his backside. A moan curled in her throat at the feel of him, his taut backside flexing with each thrust, each slam into her body.

As he stared into her eyes, Anna felt not only the quaking heat of climax rising once more, she felt an intimacy that rivaled what they'd ever shared before. Grant Ashton was her heart and her soul.

Anna released his buttocks and wrapped her legs around his waist. Grant gave a sad groan of defeat and gave up slow strokes for hard thrusts.

His hand slipped between them, his fingers dove into her curls and found her. He caressed her with quick, light circles as he pounded into her, burrowed deep into the glove of her body as he groaned and murmured her name over and over.

Tight heat wrapped her womb, electric shocks

flickered inside the heat and she gave herself over to climax once again, pumping her hips wildly with each shudder. Grant followed, his arms shaking with intensity, his forehead glistening with sweat as he rose up, cried out like an injured wolf and took his release.

Anna wrapped her arms around him, making sure he didn't leave her. She loved the feeling of his big body on hers, loved the weight of him, loved to feel the pounding of his heart against her breasts, and to listen to his breath transition from uneven to steady as he found his way back to earth.

For Grant, he felt exhausted. His body worn and his mind plagued. And yet, he wanted Anna all over again. He wanted her against the wall, in the shower and riding him. He wanted to be inside her with nothing in their way. No condoms, no boundaries. Exactly how he'd allowed himself to take her just moments ago.

A solid vise of guilt tightened around his gut. His sister's careless ways obviously hadn't stuck with him, hadn't made him irritatingly responsible today.

The chance had been infinitesimal, but nevertheless, there was a chance. For him to be bound to Anna forever.

He despised himself for feeling a grave sense of satisfaction at the thought.

"I can feel you thinking, Mr. Ashton," Anna said, her mouth curving into a concerned smile. "Do you want to talk?"

Grant heaved a gigantic sigh and rolled onto his back. "I don't know."

"Maybe just about what happened with the police?" she prodded gently.

"They believe my sister's husband killed Spencer, and that Grace was an accessory to the murder."

"What?" Anna came up on her elbow beside him.

"And they believe it was Grace and her husband who were blackmailing Spencer," he added darkly.

"But why?"

"I guess when Grace found out that he was alive and living in California, she wanted to make him pay. In more ways than one." Just walking over the information in the case again had Grant feeling punchy and ready to spring. Taking a breath, he fought for calm. "She took his money in exchange for keeping quiet about his life and his kids in Nebraska."

"Oh, Grant."

"But when Spencer stopped paying them, they went to his office to confront him and…well, we all know the rest of the story."

She sat up beside him, unaware of her nudity or how beautiful and comforting the sight of her was—or how a man, this man, would love to get lost once more in that pale skin and those curves.

Completely riveted on his account of the meeting with Ryland, she asked, "And why did he stop paying them, do you…" She stopped suddenly, her eyes going wide. She licked her lips. "You came to town."

Grant sat up in a pool of sunlight, dragged a hand

through his hair. "Sort of sounds like I'm responsible for this whole mess, doesn't it?

"God, no. Don't ever think that."

"If I hadn't come to Napa, Spencer would be alive, my sister wouldn't be wanted for his murder and I wouldn't have…"

"What?"

He reached up, cupped her face in his hands and grinned a little sadly. "I wouldn't have met you."

She leaned in and kissed him.

"Oh, sweetheart." He nuzzled her mouth. "You and Jack and the family have changed me something awful. I don't know what I'm going to do when this is all over."

"Well, first off, you're going to have to stop feeling responsible for other people's actions." She let her forehead fall lightly against his. "I of all people know how that can take over your life, your choices and your happiness."

"I'm so angry right now, Anna, I want to put my fist through a wall."

"I know. It's all right to feel out of control and angry. And it's all right to feel sad."

"Sad?"

"She's your sister, you love her, you don't want to see her—"

"No."

She pulled back, found his gaze. "No, what?"

"I'm not angry or sad because my sister might go to jail." He didn't know how Anna would react to what he was about to say next, but he owed her honesty above all things. "I don't love her, Anna. I stopped loving her the day she walked out on her babies and didn't care who raised them or how."

Tears filled her eyes. "Oh, Grant."

His throat felt scratchy, and he cleared it loudly. "I know. How could someone not love their sister?"

"My sister wasn't a saint, either. And I had to work doubly hard to separate myself from her actions. I can see very clearly why you feel the way you do."

"I tried to care for her when we were kids. I tried to understand her. God knows I did. But she just couldn't stand me or our grandparents or the life she led. She wasn't content unless she made trouble. Trouble gave her great pleasure. I tried to protect her, tried to get her to stop jumping in and out of strange men's beds, but she didn't want my help."

Anna wrapped her arms around him. "I'm so sorry."

But Grant couldn't stop. "After she left, I wanted to love her, mostly because Ford and Abigail had her in them. But..." He cursed darkly, let his head fall against her shoulder.

He wasn't a man for saying what was on his heart, showing his weaknesses, but this was Anna—his Anna—and when he was with her he felt as though he could trust her, and share the darkness of his soul.

"Ford and Abigail have you in them, too," she said, stroking his hair like a child's. "You've done good, Grant. Those two people are amazing."

"Yes, they're good kids."

"Not kids anymore. You helped them become wonderful adults."

He looked up, knew he must look like a weak calf. "They're my life, Anna."

"I know." She traced the outline of his mouth with her thumb. "Believe me I know."

"Maybe that's not right."

"It's not right for me anymore." She kissed him with all the passion of their lovemaking a moment ago. When she eased back, her eyes were wet and large and hopeful. "I've come to realize that I deserve more than just caring for others. I deserve to be cared for, too."

Grant couldn't say a damn thing and he hated himself for it. In the midst of this chaos, he didn't know what he deserved. He wasn't as enlightened as Anna, hadn't found the same understanding through their months together.

What he had found was a passion he'd thought he'd lost, a need that scared the hell out of him, and nights of confusion over where he was going.

The phone rang on the table beside the bed, and Grant gave Anna a tense look. "Am I a coward if I don't want to answer that?"

Anna's lips twitched with rueful humor. "No."

He reached for the phone. "Hello."

"It's Ryland."

Grant suddenly felt as if his chest would burst. "And?"

"It's done."

"So fast?"

"Yeah."

"You have them both?" Grant asked.

"That's right. Grace Ashton and her husband are in custody."

Ten

This time, Grant had asked Anna to come with him. And it meant the world to her.

As they whizzed down the freeway toward San Francisco that afternoon and toward a troubling meeting with someone Grant hadn't seen in decades, Norah Jones milked out a lovely torch song on the radio, while above them, the pale sun was getting lost amongst large, increasingly gray clouds.

Out of the corner of her eye, Anna watched Grant. He hadn't slept much last night, and he looked bone-weary. His fingers gripped the steering wheel, turning his knuckles white. He sat pole straight, very stiff, and the lines that etched his handsome face wreaked of anxiety and dire contemplation. She wished she could do something to comfort him, so she reached for his hand, and laced her fingers through his. Grant didn't look at her, but his back did relax against the seat and he exhaled a breath he seemed to have been holding on to for some time.

She couldn't imagine what he was feeling right now. The months that he'd been in Napa had surely been the strangest and most testing of his life. Finding out that his father was alive, being rejected by him once again, taking in the shock and the reality of Spencer's murder—then being arrested for that murder.

And now he was making his way to a jailhouse, to a cell that had once held him and now housed his sister.

As Norah belted out her final thread, Anna squeezed Grant's hand.

The walls closed in around him the moment he walked into the dimly lit jail.

Anna was beside him, her smile strong and encouraging. But for Grant, it wouldn't have mattered if he'd had his mother, grandparents and children there as well to lend their support. He felt completely alone, and very immature. His gut churned with memories of his sister, of his long, black nights in an eight-by-eight-foot cell, and the ongoing fear that he would never be released.

Surrounded by suspicious-looking cops and the smell of that sickly strong ammonia cleaning solution he remembered, Grant felt incarcerated all over again, and he desperately wanted to turn around and get the hell out of there.

But he couldn't.

Today was the last day he was ever setting foot inside this place, but while he was here he had something to finish, something and someone to finally let go of.

Wearing the same mask of impassivity he'd sported that morning, Detective Ryland met them at the front desk. But Grant could tell the man had his mind completely wrapped around this case, and the importance of its resolution. His suit looked a little disheveled and there was a rather massive coffee stain on his tie.

"You can wait in here, Miss Sheridan," Ryland said, gesturing for Anna to have a seat in the waiting room.

Anna ignored him and fixed her gaze on Grant. "Are you sure you don't want me to go with you?"

Before Grant could answer, Ryland muttered, "I don't recommend it."

"Why's that?" Grant asked him tightly.

"Your sister's pretty agitated as it is," Ryland informed him. "I don't know if you'll get the answers you're looking for with company."

"Answers I'm looking for?"

Ryland shrugged. "Personal questions, personal answers."

"Right."

"Look, we only allow one visitor in at a time anyway, but—" the detective fiddled with the paperwork in his hand "—I'd be willing to overlook the rules if you want Miss Sheridan with you."

Only a whisper of shock moved through Grant, but he stared hard and long at the man anyway. Ryland had lost his hard edge—at least where Grant was concerned. Clearly he now believed that Grant had nothing to do with Spencer's murder and was, in his own under-the-radar way, offering him a favor as another turn at an apology.

Grant looked at Anna and reached for her head, which he kissed gently. "Thank you."

"For what?" she asked.

"Being here."

"Thanks for asking me to come with you."

He nodded, a pushed smile tugging at his mouth. "I've got to do this alone, okay?"

Tears pricked her eyes and she swiped them away. "Of course."

"I'll see you in a few minutes."

She gave him a little wave and a smile. "Take as long as you need." Then went to sit in the waiting area.

Grant followed Ryland through doors and down hallways and through several checkpoints. His chest was as tight as the rest of him as he went. He could shrug off the hushed threats by the inmates he passed—their stupid comments had never gotten to him. But the cold, unflinching slam of a cell door had his muscles contracting.

When Ryland finally stopped at the beginning of a short hallway, he greeted a female guard standing sentry there, then turned to Grant and pointed to a single chair facing the bars of a cell down at the other end. It was like a scene out of *Silence of the Lambs,* but Grant refused to visit that sadistic place in his mind and memory. He turned to Ryland. "I thought I'd be talking to her on a phone in the visiting room."

The detective shrugged again. "I thought you'd want some privacy. There are no other inmates on this block, so you can say what needs to be said, ask what you have to ask, without interruption."

Grant eyed the man. "I appreciate that, Detective."

"Don't mention it." He pointed to the chair. "Have a seat. And when you're done, Officer Gerard here will take you back."

"Thanks, Detective."

"Good luck, Grant."

The ten or so feet to the brown folding chair seemed like a mile. Grant's feet felt weighted and unsteady, like walking through one of his thick muddy fields after a bad rainstorm. But just like home, he pushed onward until his fingers touched the metal back of the chair.

The first thing he noticed was Grace. On one side of the small cell, a woman in a navy-blue jumpsuit sat on the two-by-four mattress they called a bed, her back against one worn yellow wall. Her eyes were closed and she had a pair of headphones to her ears, listening to music Grant couldn't hear.

His gaze moved over her. Her appearance startled

him. She'd grown very thin and she looked as though she hadn't seen daylight in years, though the brassy blond streaks threading her brown hair tried desperately and without much success to suggest differently.

For just a moment, Grant remembered the little girl, the young Grace back in Nebraska. She'd been tan and healthy, working outdoors and eating good food. Now, she was barely recognizable to him.

Grant sat down and waited for her to open her eyes and take notice of him. She knew he was coming, he was sure of that, so it didn't take long. After about a minute, she looked up, frowned, then peeled off her headphones and sighed heavily.

"Well," she said with all the sweetness of a snake. "What do we have here?"

Her voice was scratchy and worn and Grant couldn't help but wonder if she'd ventured into more than just smoking cigarettes.

His soul dipped low. "Hello, Grace."

"Hello, brother dear."

"How are they treating you?"

"Do you really care?"

His jaw tightened. Yes, dammit. Foolishly he did care.

She pushed herself off the bed and wandered over to him, grasped a thick metal bar with one hand and eyed him speculatively. "What do you want?"

The question stopped him. He had too many thoughts racing around in his brain, too many questions. It took him a moment to sort through them and pick just one. "I want to know how long you've known about Spencer?"

She touched a finger to her thin lips. "Hmm. I've known that he abandoned us to go looking for a woman with money for about eleven years now."

"No." Through gritted teeth, Grant clarified, "How long have you known he was alive?"

Her broad smile held no warmth. "A little over ten years."

"And how did you find out?"

She sighed. "The television. He was on the news for something or other, some business deal—in the background mostly—but I knew it was him." Her eyes narrowed. "I remembered that face from the picture Mother had on her bedside table."

Grant knew the photograph well. That was exactly how he'd recognized Spencer. "I saw him on TV, too."

"And you came rushing out here, right?"

"I had to face him, to get him to answer my questions."

"And did he?" she asked as if she already knew the answer.

Grant took a deep breath, raised his brow. "God, we really are twins."

"What?"

"We have the same beginnings, but our ends couldn't be more different."

"Maybe so, but you missed out on a lot of fun doing it your way, brother."

"Did I? I'm not the one behind bars, Grace."

A slow and particularly evil grin split her features. "But you were, weren't you?"

A chill, inky-black silence surrounded Grant, then he uttered, "You knew."

She shot him a look of mock sympathy. "Shame they pinned Spencer's murder on you."

"Oh my God, Grace. You knew I'd been arrested? And you did—"

"Nothing." She shrugged casually. "That's right."

For the first time that day—maybe for the first time in his life—Grant saw Grace with fresh, indifferent eyes. She was no longer a prodigal child or a little lost lamb. She was no longer the girl he thought he could've saved. She was cold and hard and completely lost to the world. He stared at her, disgusted. "You sound like you have no remorse for what you did."

"First of all, it was Wayne who pulled the trigger. But you're right, I'm glad he's dead." She leaned in, her face almost peeking through the bars. "And I'm real glad I was there to see his fear, to see him squirm under the barrel of that gun."

"No, Grace."

"You're so self-righteous, Grant!" she shouted. "I know you and that whole bunch of Ashton bastards wanted him dead."

Grant sat forward in his chair. "No, we wanted him to pay for what he did."

She slammed her hand against the metal. "He did pay! The ultimate price."

Grant stood up, muttered gravely. "What you did was wrong."

A quick pitying laugh tumbled from her mouth and she regarded him with utter contempt. "When did you turn so soft? Oh, that's right—you always were. That's part of the reason I wanted you to take care of my kids. I knew you'd be an excellent mother to them."

Her words left no imprint on him. Absolutely none. Of all the things he'd done in his life, he was most proud to have been both father and mother to Abby and Ford.

"Make no mistake," he began, his voice dark as the grave. "Ford and Abigail were never your children. They were, and continue to be, mine."

A sweep of rage crossed over her cold eyes. "Anything else you want, brother? Did you come to try to bail me out again? You were always so good at that."

"Yes, I was good at that," Grant said tightly. "But this time I haven't come to help you save yourself. I've come to say goodbye, Grace. I've come to say I'm sorry for what you've done and I hope you can find peace."

And without another word, Grant turned and walked away, down the hall and toward the guard.

He heard Grace banging on the bars of her cell as she shouted after him, "I don't want your apologies, you little prick. And I don't want your hopes for peace." The guard nodded at Grant and led him through a doorway. "You can take all that and shove it—"

Grant didn't hear the rest. He was already out the door and walking down a far brighter hallway, if that was possible. His chest was still tight, but not with anger or grief. He had said goodbye to the past and it made him feel vulnerable, but very much alive.

When he reached the waiting room, he looked for Anna. And when he found her, he sighed. She was sitting on a chair reading a magazine upside down, her eyes glazed as if she were deep in thought. She looked beautiful, still the angel, in her white sweater, and he'd never been so thankful to see anyone in his life.

"Hey," she said, catching sight of him and jumping to her feet and rushing to his side.

He opened his arms to her and she sunk into his chest. She felt so good against him, so female and comforting. He'd never known what it felt like to be taken care of. With Anna, he wanted to.

"It's done," he whispered against her hair.

"You okay?" she asked.

"No. But I will be."

She lifted her face to him and in the middle of the jailhouse's dingy waiting room, she kissed him.

"Did I thank you for coming with me?" he uttered against her mouth.

"Yeah. Did I thank you for asking me to come?"

"Yeah."

"Good, then let's get out of here."

He grinned, took her hand and led her out of the waiting room, out the door of the jail and into the fresh November air.

* * *

The drive was quiet, but Grant held Anna's hand the whole way. Even when he shifted gears, he used her palm to do it. He just didn't want to be separated from her for a minute. And she didn't deny him that. She also gave him time to think and to grieve, commenting only on the weather and the drive, staying away from questions regarding his visit with his sister.

Damn, she got him. This beautiful woman. She really understood him. She knew he'd talk to her eventually. Knew he just needed time to process what had been said, maybe even call Ford and Abby first, and she was okay with that.

Ford and Abigail.

His mind switched gears.

Yes, he needed to call Ford and Abigail to tell them what had happened, try to explain their mother's actions and her sad future. He hoped they would turn to each other and their spouses for comfort until he returned.

And he had to return. For many reasons—his kids, the farm and the fact that he could no longer stay at the Vines. Caroline and Lucas and Grant's half brothers and sisters wouldn't want him to stay when they found out that it was his twin sister who had caused their lives to be turned upside down. He'd seen Caroline's shocked expression when Ryland had dumped the facts of the murder on the table for all to see.

His gut clenched with melancholy. Damn, he

would miss them. The whole lot of them. He'd come to regard them as family in the past few months, and it just killed him to think that they'd all end up distant and nonchalant relations.

"Hungry?" Anna asked him when they pulled into the driveway of the Vines.

"Sure."

"We could get a pizza or something."

He shoved the car into neutral and turned off the ignition. "Staying with me tonight?"

"Oh, c'mon, Ashton," Anna said lightly, opening the car door and stepping out. "You need me tonight, right?"

"I do." He wasn't afraid to admit it.

"Well, then, I'm yours," she said matter-of-factly as they walked up the pathway.

Hand in hand they went, past the house and up the stone path until they got within ten feet of the Carriage House. Once there, Grant stopped and listened.

"What?" Anna asked him, her brows knitted together.

"Did I leave the TV on? I hear voices."

"I don't know. I don't think we had the TV on. Let's go and see."

It wasn't the TV or the radio that was making all the noise inside the carriage house. It was the Ashton clan. And when Grant opened the door, he saw many hopeful, eager and welcoming people smiling up at him from the couch, the floor and all of the chairs.

Eleven

"We didn't want to intrude," Mercedes said, her green eyes bright and sincere as she looked at Grant and Anna.

Beside her on the sofa, Jared chuckled. "Well, most of us didn't, anyway."

Mercedes socked him in the arm playfully.

"The thing is," Eli began from his spot next to the fireplace, "we want you to know that we support you and that…well, we…"

"Oh, for goodness sake." Lara rolled her eyes, patted her husband's leg. "He's trying to say that we all care about you, Grant."

"That's right." Cole sat in the large armchair, a grinning Dixie on his lap. "It's been one helluva year for all of us, but we can finally put the past behind us and move forward."

Jillian, minus Seth—who was no doubt taking care of Jack and Rachel—was the closest to Grant. She reached out and gave him a hug. "Basically, we're here for you whether you want us or not."

"I appreciate that," Grant muttered as several of his siblings laughed softly at the embarrassed scowl on his face.

Over by the door, Anna watched Grant's expression. Clearly he was stunned, self-conscious and maybe even a little bit uneasy. His arms were crossed over his chest and his face looked a little pinched. To Anna, it was ridiculous, but Grant had taken this whole situation on himself, blamed himself for his sister's actions when he'd done nothing but love children that were thrust on him, protect a friend's reputation and her son's life. He was a great man, not a pariah. And yet, he'd actually expected his brothers and sisters to shun him.

Anna smiled at all of them. They had pulled together as a family and were here offering Grant only their care and support.

Recognizing his discomfort, Caroline came over, slipped her arm through his and motioned to the kitchen table. "You must be starving. You, too, Anna, dear. We brought some food and of course some wine."

"Don't worry," Cole said with a grin, helping Dixie to her feet. "Jillian didn't do any of the cooking."

"Very funny." Jillian tossed her brother a wicked glare, but he just laughed.

Anna watched as Grant's family crowded around him, talking and laughing and creating a mood of solidarity that she felt Grant needed above all else.

Caroline poured Anna a glass of wine, then set to fixing Grant a plate of food. "Now don't you worry, we're not going to stay long."

"Just long enough to give you indigestion," Mercedes said, eyeing the enormous plate her mother was making for Grant.

Caroline frowned at her daughter, then turned and handed Grant the plate. "We just felt you could use your family right now."

Grant cleared his throat, but his voice hummed with emotion as he muttered a quiet, "Thank you, Caroline."

Anna felt a sudden scratchiness in her throat and behind her eyes, and she took a sip of wine. The man she loved had experienced some hard knocks in his life, had been forced to create a family at a very young age, and had done so all on his own, with no support. He had been expected to take the burden of his sister's actions and his father's actions on himself as well, but this time, Anna thought sentimentally, Spencer Ashton had actually done something good.

He'd brought a family together.

"Anna?" Jillian called from the table. "Can you give this Tupperware lid a try? I'm all thumbs today."

Just as they had their half brother, the Ashton clan was welcoming her into their comforting fold as well. And it felt good to belong.

Anna hustled over to the table and laughingly wrestled with the Tupperware, while the men set about popping wine corks and Caroline, Mercedes, Dixie and Lara opened several baskets of food.

They stayed for just under an hour. Eating and drinking and talking about the old days when all the grown men and women around the table had been children. Strange tales of pet bees and inviting strangers to camp out on their front lawn were recounted with enthusiasm and hilarious justification. It was fun and interesting and thankfully light, and it had made Grant feel strangely melancholy. Though he was grateful to have Spencer's murder solved and the thundercloud of suspicion removed from his head, the realization that he was free to leave Napa, free to leave the Ashtons and their home, and free to leave Anna made his gut twist.

Leaving the cool easiness of the porch behind, Grant ventured back inside the now quiet Carriage House. He instantly spotted Anna standing at the kitchen counter. She was putting empty wine bottles in a brown paper bag and looking far too sexy for her own good in a fitted white tank—that incidentally had been unearthed from under the simple sweater she'd worn that day. She was long and lean, with a backside so apple-round, it made him pant.

He went to her, snaked his arms around her waist. "Well, that was pretty damn overwhelming."

She laughed softly. "I know, but I think they just

wanted you to understand that you're one of them, that you're part of their family."

"Yeah."

She turned in his arms, faced him, her smoky-brown gaze inquisitive. "What is it?"

"I don't know."

"Talk to me."

"It's hard to figure, that's all."

"What is?" she asked.

"That I have a full family, sisters, brothers and a woman who wants me to call her Mom, if I'm ever comfortable with that."

Anna slid a hand up his chest and around his neck. He loved when she touched him like that, possessive and sensual and intimate. "You don't have to ever be comfortable with that. Caroline is amazing. She's grown very fond of you, but she'll understand if—"

"No, Anna. The problem isn't that I don't want to call her that, the problem is that I do."

"And you feel you're being disloyal to your own mother's memory?"

"No." Months of tension suddenly rushed through his body. "Dammit, I'm so messed up and confused. For forty-three years I knew who I was and where I belonged. Now, everything is hazy, you know? My future and my identity are so unclear."

"I know. I'm sorry."

"I don't deserve you."

"Maybe not," she teased. "But you got me anyway."

He leaned in and kissed her. He needed her mouth

and her taste. He needed to get lost in her strength and confidence and hope to God some of it rubbed off on him.

On a soft sigh, she wrapped her arms around him and tilted her head to get a better angle, get as close as she could. They fumbled with their balance, and Grant pressed her back against the kitchen counter.

When they finally came up for air, Grant plunged his fingers into her hair and whispered, "You're going to stay with me tonight, right?"

A look of such supreme disappointment crossed her face that Grant actually felt his chest constrict.

"I want to," she said apologetically, "but Jillian mentioned that Jack was asking for me, and—"

"No, no. Sure. Of course he is." He sounded like a lunatic, and eased away from her to regain his self-control.

"He needs me, Grant," she continued to explain, as if she really needed to.

Of all people, Grant understood that children came first. But the selfish bastard inside him still scratched at its cage. He turned away from her and walked over to the front door.

"I'm sorry," she said, following him. "I wanted to be here for you—"

"Anna, you're always here for me," he said, turning back to face her. "It's about time I took care of myself."

Her face literally fell before his eyes, and he wondered if he hadn't said that last part to elicit such a reaction, to make her feel as badly as he did about a night without her. God, he hoped he wasn't that big of a jerk.

"I'll see you tomorrow," she said quickly and with a forced smile, walked past him and out the door.

"Wait, Anna."

She turned, her gaze a little cool. "Yes."

"You want me to say that I need you as well, right?"

Her brow raised. "What?"

"You want me to acknowledge the fact that I not only want you, but need you," he stated with a little too much edge. Anger and frustration needled him. It had all day, ever since he'd realized he was free to leave. And that anger and frustration wasn't aimed at Anna, but because he didn't know who to aim it at, she bore the brunt of his brusque tone.

"I'm sorry?" she said with a tightness to her voice. "I don't understand."

"It's not good enough for me to just want you, to ask you to stay the night or—"

"Grant, I know you've had a hellish day," she said defensively, "and I know you have a lot of residual anger, but—"

"Please don't psychoanalyze me, Anna."

She paused, took a deep breath and adopted a peaceful tone. "Grant, tonight is about Jack. Nothing more, nothing less."

"I don't mean tonight." He dragged a hand through his hair, turned away from her and cursed. "I'm talking about the future."

"I didn't know we had a future," she said matter-of-factly.

His jaw pulsed with frustration. What the hell was he doing? Why had he picked this fight? Why had he taken the conversation here of all places—the very place he'd wanted to avoid? Was it to get her to stay the night with him at whatever cost? Or was it to make himself be able to let her go when the time came?

"My life, my future, is back in Nebraska," he said dully.

Anna sighed as though her patience was being strained. "Okay."

"Okay?" he repeated.

"Yes, okay."

"Why aren't you fighting me on this?" he said gruffly.

"Why do you want me to fight?"

He stared at her, his heart thundering against his ribs.

"Your life is your own, Grant," she said. "Your choices, your happiness or your regrets." Her gaze softened for a moment. "I love you, Grant. But that's what this supposed future comes down to—a choice only you can make."

When he continued to stare at her, she threw up her hands. "I want you to be happy. That's all I want. But I think I've fought for this, for us, long enough. Maybe it's your turn."

She didn't wait for a response. She turned on her heel and walked out.

From the open door, Grant watched her go and felt

lonely as hell. But he knew it was a hell of his own making. If he'd wanted to send her away, make it easy on himself, he'd done a damn fine job of it.

He went inside and slammed the door. He stalked over to the table and grabbed a lingering bottle of wine, took a healthy swallow. Red current sped down his throat.

He hadn't been drunk in twenty years or more. But after the day he'd had, maybe that was about to change.

Twelve

The moon was nearly full and brighter than usual. Pale yellow light filtered in through her son's window, illuminating his beautiful baby face.

Anna sat beside Jack's crib and watched him sleep, watched him breathe in and out, watched him stir and smile. He was her family, her world, all she had left, and the urge to cling to him for a sense of security was almost overwhelming at times.

But she had never given in to her baser instincts— except maybe with Grant—and she wasn't about to do it now. Her son was not her savior or her touchstone. He was her beloved charge and her life. He was young and carefree, and he deserved the very best in life, the best mother and family.

What she had to come to terms with, Anna realized, was that Jack had real ties to the Ashtons and to Grant, and that meant that Anna would have to remain in close contact with all of them for Jack's sake. Maybe she would even check out teaching jobs in Napa when the time came, along with a few apartments in town. She had grown to love it here just as much as her son did and the thought of moving back to the city filled her with little joy.

The next few weeks were going to issue in some major changes for everyone that had been involved in Spencer's lifetime of lies. Anna knew that to keep her head above water and her heartache under control, she just had to think ahead. For Jack's sake as much as her own.

Images of Grant's intense gaze as he'd uttered a very brusque, *I belong in Nebraska. My life is in Nebraska,* rushed back to claim her. He couldn't have been clearer about what he'd wanted and what he didn't need. Yet, in his manner and look, she had sensed a real tug-of-war going on inside him. Anna didn't know if Grant loved her, but he certainly had strong feelings for her, and was actually willing to ignore them out of fear for change or a misguided sense of duty to his grown children.

She'd told him point-blank that it was his choice before walking out his door, and she was glad she had finally spoken her mind.

Anna leaned back in the rocking chair and sighed softly. She'd done the only thing she could do if she wanted to preserve some self-dignity. But that didn't stop her from wondering what tomorrow would bring, what the future would hold and if her heart would ever be able to get over the loss of Grant Ashton.

With the calming sound of her baby's rhythmic breathing, Anna let her eyes drift closed and let her mind shut down for the night.

No one ever sang, "Ninety-Nine Bottles of Wine on the Wall" for a reason, Grant thought inanely, grabbing another bottle of red and heading out the carriage house door into the cold night air. Drinking a case of fine merlot was near to impossible and for some strange reason, almost insulting to even consider.

But even so, Grant poured himself another glass of the dry red and hunkered down on the porch like a brokenhearted college boy with blanket and pained expression, and hoped that the one and a half bottles he'd consumed tonight would make him pass out soon.

He really wanted to put an end to this day.

"No one should drink alone."

Grant looked up, and through a current of chocolate and oak haze, saw Eli and Cole standing by the front door, their gazes filled with amusement.

"I thought you went back to the house," Grant muttered, noticing that his voice wavered slightly.

Maybe he was drunker than he thought.

Grinning broadly, Cole wandered over to him, sat down on his haunches. "We thought you might need someone to talk to."

"Or two," Eli added, standing behind his brother.

"Thanks," Grant shook his head, and his neck felt loose enough to fall off. "Thanks, but no thanks."

"Don't be an ass, Grant," Eli said on a chuckle. "We know how it feels to get dumped, don't we, Cole?"

Cole seemed to consider this for a moment, then shook his head. "No, not me."

A dark curse passed Eli's lips. "That's only because you've been a workaholic since grade school."

"Yeah, that's the reason," Cole said sarcastically.

Grant released a heavy sigh. "I hate to break up this trip back in time at Cole's winning streak with that ladies, but—"

"No one said anything about a winning streak," Eli interrupted. "He just said he hadn't been dumped. He only went out with one girl in junior high and high school, so there wasn't much—"

"You're rewriting history again, Eli," Cole said darkly, but his green eyes burned with humor.

"What do you guys want?" Grant practically growled.

"We're just here to hang out with our brother," Eli said.

Cole took Grant's empty glass for him. "Getting you through the rough night ahead."

"There was nothing rough about today, so there'll be no rough night ahead," Grant uttered peevishly.

"No, of course not." Eli sat down. "Your sister's in jail, you don't know if you want to go back to Nebraska and then your woman leaves you."

Cole nodded sympathetically. "That could drive a man to drink."

"No one left me, dammit!" Grant snapped.

Cole looked around. "Where is Anna then?"

"She went back to the cottage to be with Jack."

"She's such a good mother," Eli said to Cole. "Probably be a good wife, too."

"Yeah. Sweet, sexy and smart. Triple threat." Cole nodded. "I'm surprised someone hasn't snatched her up before now."

Grant seized his glass from Cole, and quickly re-filled it as he muttered something about the lack of family being a good thing sometimes.

"Jack needs to stay in Napa," Cole continued as if nothing had happened. "He's our brother after all. And that means we're going to have to make sure Anna stays here, too."

"Maybe we should find her a husband," Eli suggested, his amused gaze flickering toward Grant. "I've got plenty of friends who'd love a date with her."

"What about our CPA?" Cole suggested. "He's a good guy, fairly young and not bad to look at, if you don't mind the red hair and pale skin."

Unbridled anger bubbled to the surface, trying Grant's patience. He'd had enough of Cole and Eli. Even if it might end up being the truth, he didn't want to hear about Anna and her future with another man. On a growl of frustration, he uttered tersely, "Get out," and threw his glass across the porch like a spoiled child. The loud crash broke through his wine haze, and he watched as the pale amber glass shattered to the ground into hundreds of tiny pieces.

Eli stared at the shards of glass amongst spots of red wine and shook his head. "Mom's going to have your hide for that, Grant."

"She picked those glasses out herself, didn't she, Eli?" Cole said.

"Yes, at an antique store in…Vermont, I think it was—a few years back."

"An *accountant?*" Grant bellowed.

"What's wrong with that?" Eli asked, a mischievous grin on his face.

Cole shrugged. "He's an upstanding guy. Well, that could be the wrong choice of adjectives because he's only five-four, but he's a nice guy."

Grant looked from Eli to Cole, then shook his muddled head. "You both suck."

The men chuckled, and Cole said, "No, we're just your brothers, and this is the game we play when we want a family member to wake up before he loses it all."

"Loses what?" Grant said, frustrated.

Eli took a swallow from the open wine bottle. "Is that really a question?"

"No," Grant muttered.

"So you going back to Nebraska or what?" Cole asked, his tone serious now.

"I don't have a goddamn clue."

"Ford's married. Abby's married. What about you and your life?"

"They are my life."

"No, they *were* your life."

"You sound like Anna."

Cole raised a brow. "Insightful, too. Milton's going to owe us big-time."

Grant seethed, warned them, "If you introduce her to anyone, I'll break both your necks."

"Ah, love," Eli said, then gave a pained sigh. "Ain't it a bitch?"

"Who said anything about love?" Grant muttered.

"C'mon man, it's written all over your face. Has been for a while."

Grant scrubbed a hand over his face, hoping to erase whatever clues to his heart were written there.

Cole snorted. "Not to mention the fact that you just threatened our lives—well, our necks—if we try to fix her up."

A deep sinking feeling moved through Grant. Cole and Eli may have been annoying as hell in their attempt to make him see the error of his ways, but they were right. He didn't just want Anna, he needed her. The emotion that had his heart, had his blood pumping wildly in his veins—had him filled with excitement and happiness for the first time in a long time—was deep, over-the-top, never-going-to-recover love.

He hadn't wanted it to happen. Falling in love had been the one thing he'd avoided at all costs, the one thing he feared above all else. After giving so much, his whole life, to Ford and Abigail, he'd really believed himself tapped out. Nothing left but a tired, middle-aged man who wanted to hold on to control for the first time in his life.

But with Anna, he felt young and alive, and as though he deserved her love in return.

"You can't leave," Eli said, taking another swig of wine. "Not yet anyway. We're just getting used to the idea of you."

"How sweet," Grant said dryly.

Eli laughed, and Cole and Grant joined him.

"Marry that girl," Cole said, "and move into the carriage house permanently."

"I wouldn't be happy in such a place so small," Grant said without thinking. "I need wide-open spaces."

"We have those here, you know?"

Yes, he did know.

A loud, shrill ring came from inside the house, and Eli looked curious. "Who's calling so late?"

"Maybe it's Anna," Cole suggested with a grin.

Grant jumped up and hustled inside to get the phone. "Hello?"

"Hey, Uncle Grant, it's Ford."

Grant sobered instantly when he heard the young man's voice. He'd wanted to wait until morning to tell Ford and Abigail about their mother, until he'd gathered his thoughts and his courage before calling, but providence had intervened once again.

With a quick wave, and a few other hand gestures at Cole and Eli designed to let them know that this was an important call and he'd see them tomorrow,

Grant returned to Ford. "How are you, son? Everything all right?"

"Sure."

"And Kerry?"

"She's great."

"Good, good, and Abby?"

There was a brief moment of silence, and Grant's chest began to tighten. But Ford quickly said, "That's why I called actually—"

"She's okay, isn't she? You're taking good care of her, right? Until I can get there, and help welcome those babies into the family?"

"Well, I don't think you'll be able to get here soon enough for that." Ford chuckled. "Yep, you're a little too late, Uncle Grant."

"What?" Even Ford's laughter couldn't ease the knot of tension running through Grant.

"Abby had the babies an hour ago."

"An hour…but, it's a month too soon."

"I wish I could've called sooner, but everything happened so fast. Her water broke and, well, things just took off from there, and she ended up having an emergency C-section."

"Emergency?" Grant fairly shouted into the phone. "Is she all right?"

"She's fine. I swear. She's ecstatic actually."

"And the babies?"

"Beautiful, crying, eating, pooping—the usual. Six pounds, one ounce and six pounds, five ounces respectfully. She's just over the moon and so is Russ."

Ford took a breath, and Grant could practically hear him smiling. "I finally know what it's like to be an uncle."

The news filled Grant with mixed emotions. He was beyond relieved that Abby was okay, thrilled that the babies had been born healthy, but a deep sense of grief tugged at his gut.

"Uncle Grant?"

Grant shook his head, muttered, "I should've been there."

"You were there." Ford sighed. "You really were. In everything you taught us. Abby was so calm, so levelheaded when the docs came to tell her they wanted to take the babies out right away—and we all knew that was your influence. You're where you need to be right now, where you have to be. You'll have plenty of time to see the babies when you can come home."

"Well, it looks like I can come home soon."

"What?" Ford sounded stunned.

"There's something I have to tell you, Ford. And it's no cherry on the top of the sundae you've been eating today."

"Sounds serious."

"It is. It's about your...it's about, Grace."

For the next five minutes, Ford listened with patience and coolheadedness. As Grant laid out the terms of the blackmail and Sally Simple and his conversation with Grace in jail, Ford made no sound—and for about thirty seconds after Grant had finished. Then, in a strong, resolute voice, he said, "I'm glad this is all said and done. Everything—the case and the mystery over where Grace Ashton was and who she really is."

"I'm sorry this had to happen," Grant said tightly.

"I'm not. You were Mom and Dad to us, Grant—and I know Abby feels the same—you gave up everything for us and we love you for it. We're the better because of you, don't ever think otherwise."

Grant's throat went tight, and he didn't want Ford to hear the emotion in his voice, so he said nothing.

Ford continued, "But we want you to have what you gave us and what you made us believe we deserved all these years."

Grant swallowed tightly, forced out a gruff, "What's that, son?"

"Love."

"I have love."

"And you'll always have it, but I'm talking about the kind I have with Kerry, and the kind Abby has with Russ." Ford's voice lowered. "If you're ever lucky enough to come across it, don't let it go. Don't ever let it go."

When Grant hung up the phone a moment later, he was dead sober. And as he cleaned up the broken glass on the porch, he thought about what everyone had said tonight, about what his life had been like before he'd come to Napa, about Ford and Abby and the babies, about his mother, about Jack and Anna, and what he really wanted.

He thought about choices.

And with a full heart, he made his.

Thirteen

Anna woke up disoriented, with a major pain in her neck and shoulders.

In the white crib before her, Jack sat straight up in bed, looked directly at her and said, "Mama?"

His voice was so sweet and sleepy, her throat tightened with love. "Morning, baby."

Jack grabbed his bear and started babbling to it, and Anna stretched and rubbed her eyes. It took a moment for the morning fog in her brain to clear, but when it did, she looked around and frowned. She'd fallen asleep in Jack's room—in a hard-backed chair, no less, sometime after midnight.

The previous evening came back in a rush; Grant, pushing and prodding to hear her feelings, as if he'd wanted to know exactly where she stood, as if he'd wanted to end everything; Grace, his time in Napa and their affair in one night. And how she'd calmly and coolly told him to make that choice, make any choice, as she was done fighting for him.

Anna leaned back in her chair and sighed. She was pretty confident that her hopes for a future with Grant were over, but that certainly didn't mean she'd be able to eradicate him from her mind anytime soon. In fact, she was certain she'd dreamed about him last night—that wonderful dream that had always counteracted the horrible nightmare where Spencer Ashton tried to take her baby away. The one about her and Grant and Jack waking up on Christmas morning together, sharing presents and kisses and ideas for New Year's Day.

On second thought, maybe that was the tortured dream because it was never coming true.

Just then, Anna jumped and Jack dropped his bear as the sound of someone rapping obnoxiously on the door reverberated off the walls. Anna shifted her focus back to her baby.

"Mama?" Jack said, his green eyes wide.

Anna went to him and lifted him out of his crib and into her arms. "We'd better go see who's at the door before they huff and puff and blow the house down." And as she walked she gave him a big kiss on his belly—making him giggle madly.

Just as she reached the door and grabbed the handle, she heard Grant's voice outside, bellowing at the top of his lungs, "Wake up! Wake up, sleepyheads!"

Anna's heart dropped to the floor, but she held tight to her baby and swung the door wide. "Do you have any idea what time it is?"

"It's seven o'clock."

"That's right. What in the world are you doing—"

He shook his head. "No questions, Anna."

She just stared at him. His hair was wet, like he'd showered and ran over here, and he looked a little tired. But he was still as rugged and as handsome as ever in his blue plaid shirt and jeans, handsome enough to make her heart drop again—or maybe that was due to the fact that she loved him so much.

"Hi, Gwant," Jack said sleepily, holding his arms out for Grant.

With a wide smile, Grant took Jack from Anna and ruffled the boy's mussed hair. "How are you doing this morning, Jack?"

"Hungry," Jack said.

"Well, how about we all go out for breakfast?"

Anna quickly said, "I don't think so. We have a lot to do today." She wasn't about to revert back to their comfortable little romance. Her heart couldn't take any more breaks.

"It's just breakfast, Anna," Grant said. "Eggs, bacon, toast. Nothing long-term."

Her eyes went hot, and her throat went tight. He wasn't talking about them, but he might as well have been.

"Where go?" Jack said, touching Grant's wet hair with interest.

Grant looked at Anna. "It's a new place, but I know you're both going to love it."

"Yum, yum, yum," Jack shouted, trying to jump up in Grant's arms.

"I can fix you some eggs here, Jack," Anna said, knowing her words were going to be lost on the boy now that his big, fun brother was around.

"Will you tell your mommy that we're going for a ride?" Grant whispered in the boy's ear.

Jack grinned at her and shouted, "Ride, Mama. Eat, Mama."

Grant laughed.

"But we're not dressed," Anna began, looking down at her white cotton pajama top and bottom.

"So what?" Grant said, smiling.

She stared at him, at the two of them actually. Her son looked happy and Grant looked at home holding him as he watched her.

"Maybe you'd like to take Jack?" Anna suggested. "Have a little boy time?"

"No." Grant looked directly at her, his gaze serious now. "I want you there. And I think you know me well enough to know I won't take no for an answer."

"No, no, no," Jack said, then laughed uproariously.

"C'mon, Anna," Grant said, his mouth turning up at the corners in an easy smile. "Do this for me?"

The man made her weak. He was acting crazy and juvenile, but the sad fact was she'd go anywhere with him if he asked her. She loved him that much. But no matter what happened today, all that she'd said last night still stood.

He would have to make a choice—and soon.

Grant lifted Jack in the air and said, "What do you say, Jack?"

"Go ride, Mama. Go ride."

Anna rolled her eyes at them.

"It's chilly this morning," Grant said, so you'll both need a coat. And shoes, of course."

"Of course," Anna said with an apprehensive chuckle.

So while Grant helped Jack on with his sweater jacket, Anna slipped into her coat. "I'm hungry, too," she said, following Grant and Jack out the door. "I hope this place doesn't have a dress code."

"I assure you it doesn't," Grant said with far too much mystery.

The drive was a short one. Down the main drag a few miles, up a country lane or two and into the driveway of the house that Anna quickly realized had been the location of her Christmas morning dream.

Her heart twisted painfully as they came to a halt in front of the magnificent red farmhouse Grant had brought her to on their date night. It sat on three acres of beauty, of warmth and welcome, with spectacular views of rolling hills and vineyards—views she hadn't been able to see in the bleak light of the moon the other night. But today, this morning, with the cool November sun shining down on them, Anna saw the house well and knew that someone would make it a perfect home someday.

As they got out of the car, as Grant retrieved Jack from his car seat, Anna's gaze moved from the sweet stone pathway to the white front door to several thick fingers of ivy, scaling the face of the house all the way up to the second-floor windows. It was a magical place, where Anna felt comfortable, and it held wonderful memories within its sturdy walls and chipped paint. Memories she would hold on to forever.

With Jack settled snugly in Grant's arms, Anna turned to them, her throat tight with emotion. "What are we doing here?"

"I wanted to show Jack the house," Grant said, his gaze quietly intense.

"I thought we were going for breakfast."

"We are." He motioned for her to follow him as he walked around the side of the house, just as they had the night of their date. The stone steps felt like thick mud as she went, nervous energy making her legs feel unsteady. She didn't understand any of this, didn't want more visits to a house that she'd never live in, only dream about.

And she didn't want to feel in love and intimate and playful with a man who would never be hers.

Grant stopped just feet from the brick patio and pointed over to a large round table.

"Here we are," he announced.

Sun filtered through the wood canopy onto a table,

beautifully dressed for a meal in blue checked table-cloth, white china, sparkling crystal glasses. Anna noticed that the glasses were filled with orange juice and water and there were several steaming chafing dishes on a sideboard.

"I had a little help with the cooking, but I did set the table on my own," Grant said beside her.

Anna's gaze rested on the three place settings. There were two chairs and a very sweet, old-fashioned wood high chair drawn up to the table as though it had always meant to be set that way.

The whole scene was so odd. Fine linens and china juxtaposed against a backyard still slightly overgrown and vastly undernourished.

"Mama!" Jack exclaimed from Grant's arms.

Startled, Anna asked, "What is it, baby?"

"Turtle! Turtle!"

Anna looked in the direction that her child was pointing and saw a turtle-shaped sandbox set up on the grass, several feet away from the deck. It was clearly new, with fresh pale sand and lots of brightly colored buckets and shovels inside.

Jack squealed, yelled, "Turtle!" once more, then wriggled out of Grant's arms, ran over to it and finagled his way inside, quickly forgetting how hungry he had been a moment ago.

"What's wrong?" Grant asked her.

"Are you kidding?" she said, watching her son play gleefully with a yellow bucket and shovel.

"No."

"I'm thoroughly confused."

"You don't like it here?"

Though the sun was gaining warmth, she pulled her coat closer around herself. "Of course I like it here. Who wouldn't? But what does my opinion matter?"

"It matters to me," Grant said.

"Why?"

"Because I bought this place."

Her head whipped around so fast, her neck—which had stopped aching in the car—pulled with pain. "You did what?"

"I bought it." He sounded perfectly calm, perfectly at ease.

"When?"

"This morning. The agent was half asleep, but he perked right up when I said I was ready to buy."

She shook her head as her insides contracted with tension. "So, what? You're going to come out here to visit regularly?"

"A little more than that."

She managed a soft, "Well, that's great, Grant."

He nodded in agreement. "I'd like to go back to Nebraska for part of the winter, see my children, and my two new grandkids."

"What?"

He nodded, grinned. "Abby had her babies early." Seeing the anxious expression on Anna's face, he put his hands on her shoulders. "She's fine, great, and so are the babies. But I want to see for myself, you know?"

"Of course. Congratulations."

"Thanks."

Anna tried to ignore the sinking feeling in her belly. He had made his choice—it just wasn't her. "Wow. Babies and a new house. I'm really happy for you, Grant." And the truth of it was, she was happy for him—she only wanted the best for him and she always would.

"Don't be happy for me." He lifted his hands to her face, let his fingers dip into her hair. "Be happy for *us.*"

"Us?" The word stung her heart, and she could barely look at him, but he wouldn't allow her reluctant retreat. He practically forced her gaze to his.

"You and me and Jack," he said solidly.

Around them, a lovely breeze blew, lifting the remaining leaves on the oaks and maples toward the sky, then gently ushering them back down again. "Grant, what are you saying?"

"Sweetheart, this is our house. I want us to live here together. You and me and Jack. As a family."

Anna could barely breathe. She could barely contain the hope that was flooding her mind and heart and soul. *A family.* Something she hadn't had in so long. And with Grant, the man she adored with everything that was in her.

If she was dreaming, she never wanted to wake up.

"What about Ford and Abby and the babies?" she said with concern. "Won't you want to be—"

"I'll be there," Grant assured her. "We'll all go back to Nebraska for part of the winter. Spend a good long time."

"See the fireplace in the kitchen?"

"We'll sit by it and watch the snow fall."

She nodded. "I'd like that."

"And I'd like Jack to see his roots, and for you to see the farmhouse I grew up in."

Tears pricked hotly behind her eyes. "You know something? I don't think that's where you grew up, Grant. Not really."

He raised a brow at her, and she smiled through the tears that begun to fall. "Maybe it was this house you grew up in."

He chuckled, his eyes twinkling. "Maybe so, sweetheart." He bent his head, kissed first one eye, then the next. "I love you so much. You've made me whole again, do you know that?" He let his forehead fall gently against hers. "You've helped me realize that I wasn't living at all. I was just existing."

"I love you, Grant."

"Marry me, Anna?"

Her heart contracted and she looked up. "Really?"

"Oh, yeah." He dipped his head and covered her mouth with his own. He tasted so sweet, so right, and she hoped he'd never let her go. As if he'd heard her wish, his arms tightened around her, and his kiss turned hot and needy. She answered his silent cry, pressed her body closer, moaned into his mouth.

It was several minutes later when they finally came up for air, but when they did, Grant whispered, her lips just inches from his own, "Was that a yes?"

She smiled and nipped at his lower lip. "That was an absolutely."

"Hi, Mama. Hi, Gwant."

Looking at each other, Grant and Anna burst out laughing. Then they looked over at the baby and said in unison, "Hi, Jack."

"No go?" Jack said very seriously, holding up his bucket of sand. "Stay turtle?"

Grant turned to Anna, and with a quirk of a smile said, "No go?"

She laughed. "No go."

"You're staying, Jack," Grant called over to the little boy, his arms around Anna.

"We're all staying," Anna corrected, her heart soaring with happiness. "In this house, with this new family and forever devoted to each other."

Grant smiled. "I like that."

"And I love you," Anna replied with a smile of her own before tilting her chin up and settling in for another bone-crushing, heart-wrenching and thoroughly mind-blowing kiss.

Epilogue

Thanksgiving Day

"**T**hose pies need to come out of the oven, Jillian," Caroline said, running from saucepan to fridge and back again as she sautéed onions and celery for the sage stuffing recipe that had been in her family for generations.

"Got it, Mom," Jillian said, opening the oven.

"You have hot pads, right, sis?" Mercedes asked, her head over the sink as she peeled potatoes.

Shucking corn at the table, Lara, Eli's wife, and Dixie, Cole's wife, couldn't quell their laughter.

Looking mildly insulted, Jillian huffed, "Of

course I have hot pads." But when no one was looking, she dug in the drawer next to the sink for two grape-printed oven mitts, before rescuing the pies.

Anna stood by the wood island, slipping herbs under the skin of the turkey, smiling at her good fortune. Not only did she have the best kid in the world, the sexiest and most generous fiancé that was ever born, but a real family to celebrate the holidays with. She never thought it was possible. Especially starting out the way things had—coming to the Vines out of fear and a hope for protection, then staying out of love.

True love.

Her grin widened. She and Grant were going to be married in two weeks on the lawn just outside the cottage. After all, they'd spent so much time there and it held wonderful memories. Grant hadn't wanted to wait the two weeks, but when Anna had reminded him that Ford and Abby had to come, and the babies couldn't fly so soon, he'd agreed and thanked her for being so thoughtful.

"That turkey looks wonderful, Anna," Caroline said, admiring the twenty-pound bird. "You are a true artist."

"Thanks, Caroline. I hope it tastes as good as it looks."

"It will," Mercedes said cheerfully.

"And if it doesn't," Lara began. "The men will eat it anyway after the day they're having."

Dixie laughed. "You mean, how they're playing a nice game of football as we slave over a—"

"An ear of corn?" Jillian finished for her.

Everyone laughed. For as much as they all joked about work versus play, women versus men, each one of them took great pride in what they were doing. They loved the camaraderie of female company and had quickly embraced the traditional roles of the day. Those who could cook did, those who could not peeled, chopped and provided entertaining stories—all while the men played their game of football out by the lake—Anna's little Jack included.

A knock came from the back door, and Dixie, who was closest to it, got up.

From behind her back, Anna heard a man's voice say, "Can I speak to Anna please?"

Anna turned, saw everyone freeze when they saw Trace Ashton on the other side of the door. The young, strikingly good-looking man with light brown hair and those captivating Ashton green eyes stared somberly into the kitchen.

"Anna, someone's waiting for you outside," Caroline said with tight lips as though Anna hadn't heard it for herself.

Anna didn't know Trace very well. She'd seen him a few times, but knew the tension that was created whenever he was around his half brothers and sisters from the Vines. She thought it was about time the feud between families ended, but that wasn't up to her.

Sensing friction where there was once merriment, Anna quickly left the kitchen and followed him outside. "What can I do for you, Trace?"

He stood there for a moment, his handsome face etched with strain. "I didn't want to interrupt, but—"

"You're not," she assured him. Maybe this man had done all sorts of odious things to the people at the Vines, but he'd done nothing to her and she wanted to give him a chance. After all, he was Jack's brother, too. "Can I get you something to drink or—"

"No, I just wanted to see you, to tell you something."

"Okay." She didn't know why that would be, but was willing to hear him out.

He exhaled heavily. "Despite what you've heard, despite the terms of Spencer's will, I want you to know that Jack will always be taken care of."

The news was a bit surprising, but she couldn't help being glad for Jack's sake. It was important that he have all of his brothers' and sisters' love and acknowledgment. "Thank you, Trace."

"He's family, and so are you."

This second unexpected statement had her heart swelling with emotion. She didn't know what to say, but sadly wasn't given the chance when Eli and Cole suddenly spotted them and came around the side of the house, their faces etched with contempt.

Anna was very thankful that Jack was no doubt still down by the lake with Grant and Seth and Lucas.

"What are you doing here?" Eli asked Trace menacingly.

"It's none of your business." The reply was cool, but lacking in ire.

"Why are you all back so soon?" Anna asked, trying to deflect the situation.

"We came to see if the ladies needed our help," Eli said.

Cole's eyes narrowed. "And it looks like you do."

"No," Anna said with cool strength. "Trace has just been telling me that he wants—"

"You don't have to explain anything, Anna," Trace said. "You won't be heard by these two anyway."

Eli turned red. "I've been wanting to do this for a long time…" Fists up and ready, he moved in on Trace.

"Stop it right now!" Anna shouted, stepping between them. "You're all acting like children."

"Maybe we are children," Eli uttered darkly. "But this one here will always be daddy's favorite."

"Who cares about that now, Eli?" Anna said quickly.

Eli stared Trace down. "How could you?"

"How could I what?" Trace threw back.

"How could you be loyal to a man like that?"

Trace through up his hands. "Dammit, Eli, I hated Spencer as much as the rest of you."

Silence filled the thick air around them. The sound

of chatter inside the kitchen was the only thing Anna heard, until Cole muttered, "What?"

"Yeah, what?" Eli added.

"Believe me or not." When Cole and Eli said nothing, their faces impenetrable, Trace shook his head, gave Anna a quick nod and walked away.

The tension of that afternoon's run-in with Trace had nearly evaporated by the time Thanksgiving dinner was set before them. All the children, grown and not-so-grown sat around Caroline's beautifully dressed table, ready to eat, drink and be merry.

Grant could hardly believe that after months of insanity, he'd be sharing Thanksgiving with his new family. Jack was so excited about his new house, Ford and Abigail were coming in two weeks and staying until New Year's, and his marriage to the woman he loved was right around the corner.

He had much to be thankful for.

"You look happy, big brother." This was Eli's favorite way to address him now, and Grant was starting to get used to it.

"I am."

"I won't say I told you so," Eli said with a chuckle.

Grant shot him a sly grin. "Good."

Across the table, Anna gave Grant a sinfully hot smile, then ran her tongue over her lower lip, catching an errant drop of wine. His groin tightened and his mind fell back to that morning when he'd ravaged her in the shower, made her climax three times before lifting her up and placing her back down on his shaft. Considering her potentially delicate condition, he'd tried to be gentle with her, but as usual, she wasn't having gentle.

Her eyes remained on him, and she mouthed the words, "I love you," slowly and preciously.

"Anna's glowing tonight."

Grant couldn't help himself, and whispered to his brother, "She might be pregnant."

Eli looked surprised and whispered, "But Mercedes told me it wasn't possible."

"We thought it wasn't." Grant grinned, feeling proud as hell. "But I guess, miracles can still happen in this day and age."

"Wow. A dad again, huh?"

"Again, and for the first time."

Eli nodded, his eyes bright. "Congrats."

With a shrug, Grant said, "It's a bit premature, but I have a good feeling about it."

"Who knows," Eli said, his fork resting on his mashed potatoes. "Maybe there's another miracle— or a full-blown happily ever after—for the entire Ashton clan."

Grant placed a hunk of dark meat on his plate and sighed. "After all we've been through this year, I'm counting on it."

Eli chuckled. "Yeah, me, too."

"May sound corny as hell," Grant said, feeling

Anna's high heel brush intimately against his boot, "but life's no good without the love of those closest to you." She was staring at him, her big brown eyes dancing as she winked back at him. "No good at all."

* * * * *

DYNASTIES: THE ASHTONS
comes to a thrilling conclusion next month
with Barbara McCauley's
NAME YOUR PRICE.
Don't miss the excitement.

Silhouette®

Desire®

Trust Me

by Caroline Cross

**Imprisoned on a tropical
island by a ruthless dictator, aid
worker Lilah Cantrell finds that her
only hope for rescue is retrieval
specialist Dominic Steele—the man
who broke her heart years ago.
But can she trust him to keep
her safe…from him?**

On sale
December 2005

Only from Silhouette Books.

Tycoon Takes Revenge

by **Anna DePalo**

**Infamous playboy Noah Whittaker
gives gossip columnist Kayla Jones
a taste of her own medicine, but will
they find that love is far sweeter
than revenge?**

On sale
December 2005

Only from Silhouette Books.

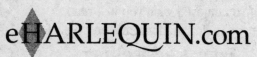

Silhouette® Desire

COMING NEXT MONTH

#1693 NAME YOUR PRICE—Barbara McCauley
Dynasties: The Ashtons
His family's money and power tore them apart, but will time be able to heal the wounds of this priceless love?

#1694 TRUST ME—Caroline Cross
Men of Steele
An ex-navy SEAL is in over his head when he has to rescue the woman who broke his heart years ago.

#1695 A MOST SHOCKING REVELATION—Kristi Gold
Texas Cattleman's Club: The Secret Diary
A sexy sheriff is torn between his duty and his desire for a woman looking for her own brand of justice.

#1696 A BRIDE BY CHRISTMAS—Joan Elliott Pickart
Is this wedding planner really cursed never to find true love—or has Mr. Right just not appeared…until now?

#1697 TYCOON TAKES REVENGE—Anna DePalo
An infamous playboy gives a gossip columnist a taste of her own medicine, but finds that love is far sweeter than revenge.

#1698 TROPHY WIVES—Jan Colley
What will this wounded millionaire find beneath this rich girl's carefree facade?